T.S. Weaver

I0745014

Cursed Blood
©Final Sword Productions LLC, 2018
ISBN: 978-1-938339-37-0
By T.S. Weaver
Layout and Cover: Sam Pray

Cured Blood is a Shadow Sprawl Novella, using the setting created by Terri Pray/T.S. Weaver.

Other works in this setting include.

Rebirth.

Alpha.

Bastet's Blessing.

To my Sam.
Thank you, now and always. Without you I'd still be writing in the dark, never willing to take the risk of sending my work out into the world.

All know the curse of the werewolves is an old one, but few know or understand exactly how ancient the legend is...

CHAPTER ONE

The woman moved with silent steps through the cool air of the temple, head held high as she met and held the gaze of those she met along the way. No one questioned her, not here, not this woman. Alena smiled, then wiped the expression from her features with a curt shake of her head.

What did she have to smile about when those beneath her care remained at risk? When her requests for aid from the city fathers remained ignored or worse, they dismissed her as if the news was unimportant.

She paused, straightening the white robes, taking a moment to prepare herself for what was to come, before she pushed the heavy wooden door open and slipped inside, away from the public area of the building. Here only those sworn to Hecate were permitted entrance, the inner chambers where the Goddess might walk among them without care, knowing her women would always be ready to answer her call.

This was where she belonged, in service to Hecate, not bound to a man in a marriage not of her choosing. She was one of the lucky ones but now that safety was at risk and she was powerless. At least in the eyes of the men who ruled the city.

Light flickered off the stonewalls, the low sounds of life in the city filtered, but were little more than the flutter of a butterfly's wings. She let her gaze move around the chamber, taking in the familiar sights as she inhaled the blessed air of this sacred place.

"They still seek to dishonor those sworn to my service," the voice rippled through the air, warm and strong, wrapping Alena in a protective blanket. *"This cannot be allowed to con-*

tinue."

Alena walked to the bottom of the statue. She didn't kneel, Hecate didn't demand such of her servants, not unless you were called for chastisement. "I have spoken with the city fathers, but they refuse to take the matter seriously, my Goddess." Her hands clenched at her sides, and she forced them to open once more.

Calm, she had to remain calm, losing her temper would do them no service. She was an adult, capable of controlling her anger, not a child who allowed her emotions to get the better of her. Alenapushed back her shoulders and kept her attention on Hecate, mentally chiding herself for letting her feelings to wander.

"A pity, they would not ignore such a thing if the request for assistance had come from Athena's priestesses."

"No, great one," Alena inclined her head. Only a fool would ignore a request from the patron of the city. She paused, framing her words before giving them life. "But Athena's temple would have sent a man with the request."

"Do you chastise me for my choice in messenger, child?" Cold, cruel, the words sucked the heat from the air for a heartbeat. With an audible sigh, the warmth returned, Hecate's words gentle. *"Forgive me, my daughter, I grow weary of the politics my kin and their servants play. Such is beneath our kind, and I fear it stretches my patience."*

Alana closed her eyes for a moment, resettling her emotions. Whatever Hecate said or did to her, she would accept it, embrace it as the wish of the Goddess. Still, she appreciated the apology, an offer few would ever expect or receive from a deity. "I am ever in your service, honored one." She opened her eyes once more and smiled. "Should you require my life, I would give it willingly. I mentioned the issue only because we now have guards in the temple, men they may have listened to. But you are right, had we sent one in my place, it wouldn't have worked." Had the message been given the weight it deserved, it would have only placed them in the same position as the others who had bowed down to the men of Athens.

Not something Hecate would ever permit.

"Better you serve me by living, Alena. I might be short on patience, but I am no fool and would never waste the life of one of my priestesses."

Alena folded her hands before her and waited, knowing there would be more to come. Hecate. Out of all the ancient gods and goddesses she could have chosen to offer herself to, Hecate was the only one she had ever heard of taking the wishes of their servants into account. "I will serve in any way you wish, from this day until the end of my days."

"I am fortunate to have such loyal servants, Alena. But if the fathers of the city will not act, then they force my hand. There are things I have held off using, but now I see no other way. My children are not toys for the men of Athens, not this day, or any other."

CHAPTER TWO

"Stay away from the temple," Petros hissed beneath his breath and took a step back until he was all but enfolded by the deep shadows of the walls around them. "You pushed too far yesterday when you decided to linger, and if they catch you trying to enter again then they'll drag you before the High Priestess, then what?"

Fool. Ophion shrugged but moved closer to the wall, despite his feelings it didn't hurt to humor his companion if only for a short while. "And why would I care what a withered old woman might say to me? She's nothing more than a female who couldn't honor her father by accepting a dutiful marriage." He kept his voice pitched low. "Besides, if I'm caught, they'll do nothing as father will protect me." What else was his father good for it, not protection? "You know how he feels about me, the bloodline, expectations of providing him with several grandsons."

Marriage, children, oh yes, those were all a part of his father's plans for him, but at least he would have a say in the woman he would marry. Not the final, of course, but his preferences would be taken into account. A luxury he knew few laid claim to while their fathers still drew breath.

He cast a sideways glance at Petros. One day his friend would learn to embrace the fortune of his station and noble birth, but it would take the return of the head of the household for it to happen. A change he doubted would occur anytime soon.

Petros snorted.

"You're getting ahead of yourself; I'm not going to get caught." Ophion continued.

"One day the Goddess Fortuna will turn her back on you. I pray, for your sake, it's not tonight." Petros warned and eased farther back from the structure. His sandals scuffed on the floor, then he paused, one hand pressed against a wall. "I'm not going in with you. Maybe you're willing to deal with the outcome of being dragged in front of the High Priestess or perhaps the town fathers, but not me. Not this time. She's powerful, all the women in service in have the blessings of Hecate, and I've no desire to be on the dangerous end of one of Hecate's curses."

A cool breeze moved through the air, tugging at Ophion's hair. "It's got nothing to do with Hecate. You're afraid of what your mother will say if you're caught." He smirked and nodded in the direction of the temple. Why couldn't Petros understand being defiant to his mother would be a means of increasing his strength?

"No, it's not that." Petros protested, a squeak entering his voice and he refused to meet Ophion's eyes. "Why would I be afraid of mine own mother? I'm a man of Athens, I control my life, not my mother."

Ophion rolled his eyes. "Why should I believe you're not afraid of the woman when you act as if you must dance to every tune. Petros, I've known you all my life, I've seen how you react when she tells you to do something. She controls the household, not you and anyone who's visited your home more than twice knows it." He paused a moment, forming his words with care, knowing what would cut the deepest. *Better to say it now, and shake him up, than never say a word and be known as the man with the fool for a friend.* "You're a coward, afraid of your own shadow. If your mother finds out you've dared to break any of her precious rules, or the rules laid out by another, she'd have you beaten. The woman forgets her place. You're no longer a child, and if your father ever returns home, she'll be the one receiving the beating. Women are supposed to be obedient to their men, not rule over them. This is Athens, the most powerful, beautiful city in existence, and in this place, women answer to men. It is how it has always been, and it's time she was reminded of this fact."

Petros paled and glanced back over his shoulder before he spoke again. "You can't say things like that about my mother. She'll hear about it. You know the slaves report everything to her. It's the only way they can avoid the extra beatings." The young man shuddered and stepped deeper into the shadows. "I'm not a coward. Fine, she's a strong woman, rules the roost, but it's not the same as being afraid. I'm careful, there's a difference."

Yes, he knew how the slaves in Petros' household acted, but he was also aware none of the household slaves were within hearing. Most would be in the villa, going about their duties, those few who might be away from the safety of the walls would be tending to brief chores, running messages or errands, and wouldn't have time to stop and listen to random conversations.

Cowardly fool.

"Fortuna is with us this night. Trust me and trust her." He nodded toward the flickering torches making the entrance to the silentÂ building. "Nothing will go wrong tonight. I have every step carefully planned and researched." He'd spend time in the temple earlier in the day, making certain he knew where he needed to be and where needed to be avoided to reduce his chances of being caught. "Trust me, Petros. This will be the greatest night of our lives. Behind those walls wait women hungry for the touch of a man, and we will be the ones to introduce them to the pleasures of being female."

"Your life, not mine." Petros shook his head and leaned against the wall. "I'm sorry. I'm not you. I'm not like you, not the way you want me to be. I should never have agreed to join you in this foolishness."

Backing out. He growled beneath his breath. He should have expected this. Petros wasn't a strong man, he'd been under the tight control of his mother for far too long now. Perhaps it was too late to help his friend find his strength and step into the role of manhood. "Fine. Return to your home. To your mother and your slaves. I'll tell you all about it tomorrow if I feel generous enough. But it won't be the same. You'll never know what it's like to touch one of the handmaidens with your own fingers. To taste their sweet lips and feel them shiver in your arms. They are the maidens of Hecate and who knows what secrets they may impart when they lay without the arms of a real man?"

"Hecate may..." the words trailed off the other man closed his eyes, shaking his head before he continued. "No, there's nothing I can say that will change your mind. Of course not. You plan on going through with this foolishness."

Foolishness? How could I ever have named this boy my friend? His hands clenched, the need to strike out, to teach Petros a lesson, exploded into life, tightening muscles and nerves alike. "No, there isn't." He grinned, burying his anger. "They're waiting for me, I can feel it. The women who serve Hecate know when something important is about to happen, even my father agrees they are blessed by the divine. A blessing they must be taught to share, and not keep to themselves." He moved away from the wall to take a better look at the entrance.

"Take heed of my words, please, and rethink this night. Don't ruin it all by taking this risk." Petros pleaded but made no move toward him. "You can find other pleasures. Other adventures. Ones which will not result in you being cursed for the rest of your life. I'm begging you not to do this."

Whining fool. Weak. If he would take hold of his manhood and do this with me, he would be able to cast off the fears which now ruled him.

Cursed Blood

Torches flickered, casting deep shadows across the triple-faced statue guarding the entrance to the marble-clad walls. How many slaves had it taken to build the structure? Where bodies buried in the walls? Blood mixed into the sand? Not that it mattered, their work had been in service to the gods, and their masters' were the important ones. They were, after all, only property which could easily be replaced in any slave market.

Or at least some of them could be.

The skilled ones were different, those were taken care of, their tools locked away when the slaves weren't using them. They were granted small luxuries when their owners believed they had earned such things, but they were still property at the end of the day. Bought and sold on the whims of their betters. Slaves who answered to a master and had no say in their lives.

The same as it should be with a woman. Oh, there were families in Athens who knew how to control their females, keeping them within their homes until the women were handed over in marriage to the right man. Yet these women who served Hecate acted as if they were better than any man. His jaw tensed at the idea. They would learn their place, no matter if it took him the rest of his life to teach them.

"Be safe," Petros spoke but left before Ophion could tear his gaze away from the temple. "And return home in one piece."

He'd regret his decision. When Ophion had finished his adventure and retold the tale a dozen times over, then Petros would voice his regret over not taking part in this nights foray. Oh, the stories he would have to share with his friends once he returned home.

Now, before the guards' return. Before it's too late.

He waited for the count of three rapid heartbeats, long enough to be sure there was no one else in line of sight who might witness his actions. A long moment later he was at the side of the steps, pressed against the cold stone, heart racing, sweat beading across his forehead. There was another way in, one used by the maidens and those in service, which would help him avoid the main steps. He smiled at the idea. Chance alone had allowed him to discover the hidden entrance and made the entire plan workable in the first place, assuring him Fortuna's hand still rested upon his shoulder.

After all, if the Goddess of luck weren't on his side, he'd have never discovered the carefully placed doorway.

With a quick glance to assure himself, he was still alone, Ophion moved along the side of the temple, counting the blocks of stone the way he had observed others do.

Eight. Nine. Ten. There...

The small change in stonework confirmed he'd located the right place.

He pressed two fingers into the small, hidden, indent and the stone shifted. He tensed, the grating sound carrying more than he believed possible in the quiet night air. If anyone else reacted to the sound...No, he couldn't think like that, not when he was close to success.

Nothing.

Not even the cry of the watch which had been imposed on the city in recent days. Odd, he still didn't know the reason for the change -- his father, when asked, had announced it was not Ophion's concern -- and Ophion had been left to take his anger out on a slave. He was a grown man. He had a right to know what was going on in the city. Perhaps, after this night, he would be able to convince his father he was truly a man now, not in years, but ability.

All this to prove my worth to my honored father? So he might look on me with pride instead of barely seeing me at all?

No, there was more to this than proving himself a man to his father, or anyone else. This was about his own desires and the way the women he'd met, acted. He'd watch, for weeks now, before making his decision to enter. The more time he'd observed the women, the greater his desire to teach them the meaning of being a woman in Athens, had become.

They desire this. The way they flaunt themselves, how they move. This is what they want, what they wish.

He eased the stone aside enough to allow him to enter, took one last glance around before he slipped inside. The rock scraped back into place, though he had no idea how it worked. Had there been an extra piece of the mechanism he'd triggered to close the stone portal?

What if he couldn't get it to open when it was time to leave?

I'll escape another way, and I'll find out how to use the door another time.

Ah yes, of course, if things worked out this wouldn't be the only time he took a chance to sneak into the temple. The maidens of Hecate, unlike those of Hestia, we're trained -- according to rumor -- in the erotic arts. Odd, he would have assumed those sworn to the service of Aphrodite were taught the delights of such skills, but he'd been quickly disabused of the notion.

Be honest, the priestess slapped me.

Yes, she had, and with far more force than he'd have given the young woman credit for had he not been on the receiving end of the blow. Women had no right to lay their hands upon him, not in violence at least. Yet she had struck, without hesitation, her words sharp and meant only for him before she'd turned and vanished into the safety of the building.

His jaw clenched. No, he'd find a way to teach the woman a lesson, but not tonight. This time he would focus on the women in Hecate'sservice, a practice run before he laid plans to exact his revenge on Aphrodite's women.

He touched the sides of the short tunnel, searching for his way out. It didn't take long to walk through the narrow passage and exit out into an open section where he peered out into the main body of the temple. Where, exactly, was he? All he could see were columns clothed in shadows.

Alright, that meant there had to be a light source if he couldn't see where it was coming from. Lamps or torches? He eased his way out from behind an intricately carved stone. Lamps, it had to be. The gentle warmth of the glow beckoned in the distance, but it didn't help him figure out where Â he found himself.

A part he'd never seen before? It would make sense. Any secret entrance would lead into a private part of the temple, to reduce the chances of being discovered by those who entered this place as supplicants.

He rolled his eyes. If you were going to kneel before a deity, why choose a woman? Why not Ares? Or Zeus?

Something moved, a flicker of shadows in the shape of what? A woman? Had he entered the right part? Was the female a priestess or a servant bound in service? There was no way of telling from his current hiding place.

He chewed on the inside of his cheek, uncertain. Then moved farther into the building, keeping close to the walls. He didn't want to be caught, not this quickly, preferably not at all. Once he found a woman, and introduced himself, shown her the pleasures he could offer, then all would be as it should be.

He was, after all, not unskilled in the gentle arts of Aphrodite. He'd had slaves enough to practice on and paid for -- on rare occasions -- time with more knowledgeable women. Not a detail he would share with the women, as it was none of their concern. But he had enjoyed the lessons he'd purchased, and the handmaiden would have no room for complaint by the time he was done with her.

The female figure moved into the next chamber, and he followed her to the opening into the room before he peered around. What was she doing up this late at night? A sacred rite? Or a restless sleeper?

The woman was alone and would work for what he had in mind.

The female stood, wrapped in her robe, before an altar though he knew it wasn't the same one supplicants were taken to when they wished to make an offering to Hecate. He'd spent time exploring in the guise of such a being and didn't recognize the room. The statue; no denying who it represented. Like the ones he'd come across before, it served Hecate, though here only one of the faces was truly visible, the other two remained in the shadows, protected by the deeply carved cowls, as if of lesser importance. Three bright lamps had been placed around the base of the statue, adding to the warm glow illuminating the chamber, but the scent rising from the oil was off and unfamiliar to his nose.

He inhaled again, needing to learn, to understand what he faced. Yet knowledge eluded him.

Strange. There must be a reason for the aroma. Is it found pleasing to their Hecate, or is it a form of cleansing? He could ask the woman he chose for the night. Still, he wanted to know what had been added to the oil? He tasted the addition, trying to place the aroma only to shake his head. Heady, but pleasant, it tempted him to breathe in more. A spice? But why would anyone in their right mind add spice to lamp oil? It didn't make sense, but then again when women were involved, foolish things happened. Silks wasted in decoration, perfume on pillows, decorative shells and other items scattered to make a room more pleasing to the eye. None of it made sense to him, but females were curious creatures at the best of times.

Ophion tried again, determined to identify the scent but his brain refused to surrender the information, and he blinked, trying to force his mind into order. The figure of the woman in front of him wavered, her shape no longer solid as he stared at the robe-clad form.

What's happening? He frowned and rubbed one hand over his eyes. His ability to grasp thoughts and sort through them, no longer worked the way it was supposed to. He blinked, but it didn't help. Something pressed down on him, restraining his ability to think clearly.

The spiced oil? Could it be the smoke from it was now affecting his ability to reason? No, it had to be more, he wasn't a weak-willed fool who fell prey to tricks. If the oil was the cause, why wasn't the woman affected?

His skin tensed across his left shoulder, prickling, goose flesh forming until the hair across the back of his neck lifted, and he paused. A hand. It took a moment to register the change in pressure, the sense of fingers touching between his neck and arm. Touched, he was being affected.

His gaze narrowed, focusing long enough to make out the form as he turned to stare at the newcomer. A woman, older, wearing a black trimmed robe, face bared, her grey touched hair loose around her shoulders save for a knot pinned at the back of her head. Her thin lips pressed together, creases deepening around her mouth and eyes.

"You don't belong here."

Ophion opened his mouth to protest, tried to speak, to say something as he shrugged in an attempt to shake off her grasp, but his body refused to respond to him. His knees weren't working, a fuzzy awareness taking their place. His limbs heavy, chest tight as the woman took hold of his chin in her free hand, bone-thin they pressed into his flesh, yet the pain he knew should be present, didn't register.

"You. Do not. Belong. Here." Her face inches from his. "Sleep."

His body obeyed.

Ophion turned, shaking his head, blinking again in an attempt to clear his vision.

"It is done, honored one." The High Priestess, Alena, bowed her head before the statue. Had they done the right thing? The curseHecate wished to use was a powerful one, it's like never seen before, at least to the woman's knowledge. Fear knotted in her belly at what it might do to the captive, but it wasn't her choice in life. She served Hecate, not the other way around. "He has been detained for a time in the caverns below." Unconscious the boy had been a dead weight, and it had taken three of them to shove the intruder out of the chamber and into the cells.

The statue moved, barely a fraction, but enough that Alena knew the power of Hecate infused the stone once more. *"He will pay the price, as will any others who dare to enter this place with darkness in their hearts, and lust for one of my daughters. I will no longer tolerate such disrespect and evil within my home."*

"As you command, my Goddess." Had other women found themselves put to the foul use of men in temples? Rumors persisted, she had tried to avoid them, but they remained active through the market place. Unavoidable even if she had attempted it.

"You do not approve of my decision, daughter mine," Hecate chided, her voice gentle.

"I worry how the curse may act out. How it might taint others," she bowed her head, lowering her gaze to the stone-clad floor. "It would not be necessary if the father's of the cities listened, and brought the young men under control. You are, of course, correct this must be handled once and for all, honored one. I only wish it had never come to this point."

"On that, we agree. But when the city father's refused to listen, what other choice did we truly have? I have placed warriors,

guards in my home, and yet these cruel men continue their dark plans. Seeking entrance with only cruelty in their hearts."

The Priestess had no answer, and folded her hands and waited for Hecate's instructions. Her sisters were, for now at least, safe from the intrusions of one young man, and word would spread that the Goddess would protect those who were sworn to her. Or it would once the spell was released on the male, and others bore witness to the result of defying or attempting to defile those under the protection of the goddess.

"It was a powerful spell," Hecate mused, the statue shimmering as all three heads turned to face the waiting woman. *"One we will watch over. If all goes according to plan, it will be contained to the home of this one, ignorant young man."*

And if it didn't, there would be ways of containing it. "Perhaps it is right that the punishment spread beyond the single family. Many others are involved in mistreating those in this home," Alena mused, though the idea sickened her. The punishment of one was seldom enough if the others involved were of a mind to ignore such things. Yet this spell, the plans Hecate had built, was far more dangerous than Alena had ever born witness to, and for now, it remained contained until Hecate released it upon the boy. "If the other families had done their duty and taught their sons respect then this situation wouldn't exist in the first place." It was the wealthy families who had failed the city, those who believed themselves above both custom and law. Some had tried to blame the incidents on those who lacked the funds to protect their kin, but the priestesses knew better.

"The boy will return to his home; he will be too wrapped in agony to leave. His weakness exposed to the world. Perhaps he will begin to feel my displeasure before he is released, perhaps not. Only time will tell. It should be fully released once the moon rises and he is within my power."

Alena closed her eyes and tried not to think about the women in the home. There would be causalities, and it was the choice of her Goddess if such happened. Slaves, daughters, mothers, aunts, who knew how many women remained in the walls of the villa? "What of the women? Is there a means of protecting them from the curse?"

"If the women survived, they would then be blamed for the curse, and their deaths would be public, humiliating and painful far beyond the death offered by my touch. You know how women with power are viewed if they are not already in service. Then you are seen as women who have forgotten their place and duty to their families, despite the respect once given to those who entered the temples. This is our only option."

She wanted to believe it, needed to, her faith in Hecate absolute. There were other options, ones those of Olympus were prone to calling upon. The Furies. The devastation of an entire city. Playgrounds of the gods, painted with the blood of mortals.

"My kind are not perfect, sweet one. Despite what my brothers and sisters might prefer humans believe." The sigh audible. *"It is unfortunate our mistakes can be more powerful than those of a mortal, and we must be careful of what we do, where we unleash our powers. This is not an action I take without careful consideration, now I wonder if it is the right decision, but I find myself lacking options."*

The Priestess kept silent. This wasn't the first time Hecate had indicated the Gods were as prone to mistakes as the men and women in her care. An idea which would be rejected beyond these walls, though she had nothing to do with those in service of the other gods and goddesses and couldn't know if they had been told the same thing. She doubted it with certain members of Olympus, Ares, Zeus, and Poseidon came to mind, but a few of the others might have mentioned it.

"Whatever happens honored one, we will remain in

your service."

CHAPTER THREE

Ophion groaned and tried to open his eyes. Thick crusts of sleep cracked and crumbled under protest until he blinked. Light stabbed at him, and he closed them once more. His head pounded, and he swallowed, throat dry. Had he been drinking with his friends? Too many skins of wine and other things. Except that didn't feel right.

Memories came to his call reluctantly, but then, he wasn't sure what had happened.

No, he hadn't been drinking. The plan had focused on other things, but his mind remained swamped with a heavy blanket, keeping him from being able to find the answer. A little longer, that's all he needed, a rest, a few deep breaths to clear the remaining fog, then he would be able to deal with the remains of the hangover. He lay, eyes closed, his breathing slow, as he let the sluggish weight in his head, shift and dissipate.

Despite everything, the memories he had forced to the surface, the headache, dry mouth, and rolling stomach made no sense as he'd only ever experienced such from indulging in too many cups the night before.

How much did I drink, and when did I find the time?

Had he found wine in the temple? It was possible. Wine was often one of the offerings made to temples, which meant there would be enough of it lying around.

Why couldn't he remember the woman he'd passed the evening with? He'd spent many a night planning things out, searching for an entrance, and he could recall the feel of the stone beneath his fingers. The way it had moved when he'd found the right one and pressed in, but now everything else appeared locked away, held back where he could no longer reach it.

Ophion stretched or tried to, but something jerked him to an abrupt stop. He attempted to part his wrists again, but the same thing happened, confining his wrists in front of him. Cold, hard and unyielding despite the way he pulled and tugged on his wrists in an attempt to force them apart.

He glared down at his hands, confusion adding to the remaining confines of his sleep, and yanked. Hard.

Metal clinked against metal, heavy bands around his wrists as his mind struggled to force order where chaos now reigned. Cold shock followed the realization.

Chains.

Ophiongrowled and tried to free his wrists again, but the chains were strong, well-formed, and without a key, he couldn't imagine a way of breaking free of them. He simply wasn't strong enough, and the knowledge only added to his growing frustration.

Water, he needed water if he would ever speak again. His tongue stuck to the roof of his mouth when he tried to make noise again, thick and heavy. He blinked and tried to force his eyes to work, but the blurred edges of his vision remained in place, and he rested his head back on the bed.

He rolled his eyes at the idea. Some bed it had turned out to be. The pallet was nothing more than a ticking stuffed sackcloth, rough and barely adequate for a slave, let alone one of his blood. Especially now he understood it was laid directly on the floor instead of being lifted on a wooden platform. Not a covering of fur or sheepskin to protect his body from the chill. And, now he was awake, his bones protested the cold seeping into his bones in the dim cell.

Cell?

No, that couldn't be correct. He frowned and tried to sit up as he took in the chamber. A door, heavy at first appearance, and the only light appeared to be coming from outside the room. A small lamp, or a torch?

He tried to stare at the light, but his eyes protested, and he looked away. Torches from how the light flickered as lamps were generally protected from drafts. The smell suggested wood in the mix, which added to his belief the illumination came from simple torches in sconces. Which meant he was not in a part of the temple used by many, as torches were also more prone to being extinguished. It didn't bode well for him or his situation. It didn't matter what he tried to tell himself, but he was confined in a cell, locked away, and bound in chains.

Was there anyone beyond the closed door?

Only one way to find out.

"Hello?" He called out and tried to move his feet, rolling to his hands and knees before he was finally able to make his way over to the door and pulled himself upright. "Anyone out there?" He pressed his face to the small, barred opening and scowled.

Nothing. Not a damned thing. No sign of life, not unless he counted a spider building a web between two of the bars.

No, they couldn't have left him on his own. He was important. His bloodline was old and respected. If no one had recognized him, his clothing alone should have given away his status. So, why was he locked up in here, alone, with no one in shouting distance?

Who in the name of Zeus believed they had the right to restrain him like a common slave? Didn't they know who he was? Who his father was? He growled and tried to sit up but his balance refused to comply, and it took him several moments before he managed to force his uncooperative body into a seated position. He was of a noble house, he was supposed to be protected from such abuses, and he'd committed no crime to be locked in chains.

Maybe a small one, but nothing that deserves this. I belong in a small private chamber, perhaps with lightweight chains, but with a bed, blanket and anything else due my rank.

He couldn't be certain entering the temple without permission was an actual crime or more like a break in custom or at worst a minor offense. Either way, the point should have been brought before the city fathers or directed to his own father instead of the women treating him like this.

Did they do it? The place wasn't home, he knew that much from the background aromas and the lack of familiar sounds.

Instinctively he tried to open the door. Pointless, the door remained closed regardless of how hard he pulled on it. Unsurprising, what would be the point in placing a chained man in a room with an unlocked door. Still, women were weak and might have panicked, or believed the chains enough to hold him in place.

"Hello?" He tried again and pressed closer to the opening. "Can anyone hear me? I'm awake. I need to talk with whoever is in charge. "There had to be a guard, a watcher, servant, a person who would run and get the woman in charge. It wouldn't make sense to leave him completely alone. No one would know when or if he awoke.

Unless they don't care if I ever wake up again?

Cold sweat beaded down the length of his spine and he swallowed down a hard knot of fear. How long had he been left in the cell? What had caused him to blackout? There'd been a scent from the oil lamps. Wrong, heady, and touched with spice. Could that have been the cause? It was the only thing he could think of, he'd felt nothing else, except the wall on the outside, but a drug on an outside wall would be dangerous, too many people walking back and forth, increasing the risk of someone accidentally coming into contact with it.

Had to be the lamps. No dart had pricked his skin, and he'd drunk of neither wine nor draft.

But why hadn't the oil affected the woman? It was one of a hundred small details he tried to force into a semblance of order.

Where did they get the drug from? Perhaps he could find out, if they kept him here much longer, what had been added to the oil. It was a detail he could use -- and he'd be a complete fool if he ever believed there was a remote chance the Priestess would share the information with him. Why would they give up one of the rare advantages they had when it came to dealing with men?

He growled then rested the back of his head against the door.

"There has to be someone close who is listening to me. Ignoring the fact I'm awake will only make matters worse when my father finds out. You don't want to upset him, or the city fathers, do you?"

They mean to let me die in here. Gods, my father will never know what happened to me.

No, it was a foolish idea. What would it gain the priestesses? Petros knew where he had gone and would, if pressed, reveal his intentions to Ophion's father. Those serving here could not simply leave him, abandon him in this cell, to die. For all, they knew he had told a dozen different people his plans and would be missed.

Trouble the temple couldn't afford.

Patient. All he had to do was sit and wait. At most he'd be kept here until dawn. Waiting wasn't such a hardship.

Except for the cold.

His bones ached as he slid into a sitting position, his back against the door. Damn women, they hadn't left a blanket in the room for him but must have known how the cold would affect anyone left in the cell. He tried to rub his hands over his upper arms, but the chains made the movement difficult, though not impossible.

Cruel.

A fair punishment in their eyes? Taking the law into their own hands. *For what? All I did was explore, not as if I had the chance to touch anyone. Besides, it's a rite of passage to break into a place like this.* At least, it's what the rumors spoke of. Tales from those older companions who had crossed into manhood a few years ahead of him had been all too eager to share stories of slipping into forbidden places.

"Do you wake?" A soft, feminine voice came from behind the closed door. "Boy? Do you wake or was the noise nothing more than the wind seeking to cause problems?" Her tone sharpened, lacking compassion.

"I'm no boy, but a man grown." He growled the worlds as he pushed back to his feet, turned and glared through the bar covered the gap in the door. "I'm Ophion, of house..."

"Your house and lineage are of no concern here, child. It is your actions; we will judge you by." The woman interrupted him. "The Priestess will see you now, but you must be silent until she gives you permission to speak if you would ever dare speak again." Metal scraped against metal, the sound grating through his bones as the lock opened. "Step away from the door, boy, so I might open this door in safety."

"My name--"

"Is boy, until the Priestess says otherwise, now step away from the door or you will remain here another night, and another, until you learn to do as you are told." The woman didn't shout, but her words carried into the cool air of the cell.

She wouldn't dare.

Yes, of course, the female would. This was not the type of threat a woman made unless they could back up their words with force and authority both. Did the temple have warriors protecting it? He'd never seen one, but he was no longer sure he'd explored the place enough during the day to attempt his infiltration. He growled beneath his breath, closed his eyes and forced himself into silence.

If he pushed now, he would find himself locked in the cell until it pleased the woman, or one of her sisters, to return to him.

Long, deep breaths marked the passage of time as he brought his emotions under control.

"If you remain silent and obedient, your life will become far easier during your stay here. You are now in the realm of Hecate, boy, and here your family, your wealth, and your dreams mean nothing."

His jaw clenched as he edged away from the door, turned and faced the woman. A cowl and shadows covered her features, allowing him only a glimpse of chin and lips.

The door opened, and he tried to see more of her as she stepped back from the entrance. "You are under the gaze of Hecate and her priestesses, and it is known her eyes miss nothing. A fact you would do well to remember."

Ophion didn't move. He could play this game, make the female believe he was now cowed and obedient. They didn't know him, didn't understand he was able to twist women to his whims, then strike when least expected. A skill he had put to use more than once. For now, he would paint on the face of the quiet, obedient man and wait for the right moment.

I will win. They can't stop me, they have no power over me.

"I see you understand. Now follow me, and know we are watched. Always watched within these walls. Should you make the wrong move, attempt to harm any of us, you will be punished for it as I have said. The Goddess knows all, sees all." The woman stepped aside and waited for him to leave the cell, gesturing with two fingers when he stood, silent, watching her. "You will speak truly, regardless of your desires to do otherwise. And you will wish to lie, all men do when faced with Hecate. The truth alone will either condemn you or set you free, depending on the wishes of the Priestess and Hecate herself."

Ophionlifted his head and forced himself to walk out of the cell. The chains securing his ankles made taking his normal stride, impossible. Metal clanked against metal, and he stared at the links binding his wrists. Why could the woman not free him from the bonds? Did it make her feel stronger to see him restrained as a criminal or slave might be?

"The Priestess has much she needs to discuss with you, boy. She will want to know what brought you to our home, and it is best you know she is able to tell when a man, woman, or child, lies to her. Hecate herself has blessed the Priestess with this gift." The woman bowed her head as she named the Goddess, but the movement was brief, nothing which he could use to sleep free or attack his guard.

Besides, if she had given him a chance, the woman had made it clear they were being observed. If he attempted to strike down the woman or overpower her, the alarm would be raised and all would then tumble out of control for him. It was one thing to sneak in and spend time with the women here, it was another to strike down one of their number with witnesses left to recount each sordid detail.

No, better to wait until he had spoken with the High Priestess, and make the woman see sense.

"This way, boy," the woman opened a door at the end of the corridor and led the way up a flight of stone stairs. She didn't hurry, perhaps she considered the reduction in his stride. "Remember my warning, young one. Speak not until she gives you leave too." She stopped in front of a closed door and turned to meet his gaze as her cowl slipped back from her face.

His heart skipped a beat. Brilliant blue eyes met his, fearless, proud and secure in her power and position. His body hardened beneath his clothes and he struggled against the urge to step closer to the woman. Her beauty called to him, as it did every time he met a woman with the same type of raw, undeniable grace, it was a woman like this one who drew him to the temple. She was proud, arrogant and needed to learn her place within Athens.

Women answered to men, to the males of their family, in the city. If they had no family, then the wise ones found a man to exchange protection for sex, those without guardians were prey to the men who called the city home. It was the nature of things and always would be, and yet these priestesses acted as if they were better, stronger, above the rule of men and in control of their own lives.

A foolish idea.

She will learn. Once I'm free of this and have spoken with my father; she and all the women here will know, will learn what it means to treat one of my standing in such a manner.

"You are not in command here, boy. Keep that always in your heart and mind when you meet the Goddess, and you will have a better chance of walking out in one piece."

His jaw clenched. How dare this woman talk to him like this. She would learn. They all would. If it took him the next full year to meet out his vengeance. No mere female would ever have such power over him.

"Enter, child, and kneel in the circle of light." A new voice, strong, older but still feminine called from the new chamber.

No, not new, it was the same one he'd entered earlier, where he'd seen a woman standing before a statue and had collapsed when an older woman had confronted him. Ophion frowned but did as he was bid, and walked into the chamber, head held high, taking note of the statue once more. Like before, only one face of the carefully carved marble appeared to be fully formed, the other two remained hidden in the stone cowl shadowed her features.

In front of the statue, her back to the door, a woman in the robes of the High Priestess stood. Waiting for him? Or in communion with Hecate.

His gaze shifted to the circle of light. Kneel? Why would he kneel? They were women and meant to follow the lead of men, but in taking service with Hecate, they had found a means to avoid the proper control of their families. Perhaps these women had been cast aside by their own people and ordered into the care of the temples. It wasn't unheard of for female children to be left, exposed to the elements, or handed to temples, or sold if a family needed money. Who wanted too many girl children in a family?

The Priestess didn't turn but remained silent in front of the statue.

Waiting for him to kneel, an act he had no interest in completing. *But I have to if I want to be free of this place. I have to obey them, play the subdued male, seeking forgiveness. An act, a game I need to complete if I wish to return home.*

Silently he stepped into the circle of light, the soft chink of the chains between his wrists reminding him he was the prisoner here, his rank meant nothing to these women and, as such, he would have to push himself to obey the women regardless of the cost to his pride.

When he was free, away from this place and back in his family's villa, he would find a means to strike back, to gain such revenge that the women of Hecate would never again think to flaunt themselves, to claim a position of power over the men of Athens.

Silently, nursing his anger, Ophion knelt.

The Priestess smiled, her back to the boy. His anger

rippled through the air, a living, breathing thing he refused to control. A pity, the time in the cell had done nothing to teach the intruder a lesson. A better man might have understood, accepted his actions and apologized for entering the temple with evil in his heart.

But this was no man, despite his claims otherwise. A boy who believed himself above the woman and her sisters. Above the teachings and protection of Hecate, and now he would learn.

A warning she hoped never to repeat.

"He will learn, as will his friends. This story will spread, and my daughters will be safe again." Hecate's voice whispered through her mind. *"The city fathers should have listened to you, my child. They didn't, and they will pay the price. I will no longer allow what mine to be mistreated by them, or their sons."*

Alena smiled, though it didn't warm her. Ice wrapped itself around her heart, and she waited, knowing the boy was behind her, impatient. He didn't like the silence, being forced to kneel, to be subservient to a woman, Goddess or not. His pride was a part of the problem. His belief all women were here to be entertainment for him, and those of his kind.

"It will take many years before men finally accept women are not their playthings, but we will try to teach them, and I will protect those who are mine. But I must start with this one, the first of these foolish boys who would turn my daughters into their slaves."

A small noise, a shifting of weight, enough to alert her to a growing impatience coating the young male. Would the curse be needed? Perhaps a show of power would work instead? No, she'd had this discussion with Hecate, and once the Goddess had set her mind to a decision, she didn't walk away from her choice without reason. Without proof, the initial decision had been a poor one.

It is time. We will show him the way.

CHAPTER FOUR

The cold stone beneath his knees stole away what warmth remained in his chilled body, and he shivered. How long did the women expect him to wait here? To stay on the stones as if he were nothing but a servant or slave? He had other things to do. A home to return to, revenge to plan against the foolish females. The idea alone was the one thing which kept him from growling at the back of the silent woman.

Patience. It will be done with soon enough. She will grow bored, turn and talk with me. Then I can return home, to my bed, to the comfort of some women who know their place in life. Women who understand service. They would wear the collar and chains of slaves, the only important detail would be their obedience.

"Your pride and anger threaten to get the better of you, though a man with any sense would use this time to contemplate what he had done and why those actions were wrong. How you offended the Goddess." The Priestess sighed as she turned to face him. "You prove in your silence, that you are not yet a man ready to face and accept the wrongs he has done to others. No, you are a boy who has yet to learn the values of patience, humility, and respect."

Ophion'sjaw tensed.

"Anger, even now." The woman glanced at the door behind Ophion. "You entered my home without permission, after our doors were closed for the night, and used an entrance which is restricted to those who serve here. Those sworn to Hecate." The woman took a step toward him. "Not a position of honor you can claim, no matter what lies you might have told yourself."

No sound. Not a swish of cloth, or a footfall. His breath

caught at the back of his throat. How was it possible the woman moved without noise? Hecate's magic?

"That action alone would be enough to earn you a public whipping. But the hidden reason for your visit, the one the Goddess warned me about, is a far more serious offense. One we cannot allow to go unpunished."

What is she talking about?

"Your plan to befoul a handmaiden of the Goddess-Hecate. The reason you entered this place was to commit evil upon one of the women here." Her voice hardened.

Befoul? What was the damned female going on about? He'd merely planned on... Ophion blinked and stared at the priestess. He'd not said a word, planned but not actually spoken. How had she known what he'd been thinking? Or had she found Petros and persuaded him to talk.

Petros was many things, but strong wasn't one of them. With the right pressure, Petros would have spilled everything, and if he had betrayed him, the Ophion would no longer name him as a friend. Such a betrayal could not be easily forgiven.

"Then I will put this in simple terms. You entered this temple with the single-minded desire of taking a handmaiden of Hecate and using her for your foul pleasures. Is this not true, boy?" Her voice a cold slash across his throat.

He swallowed down his fear, allowing anger to take its place. "Foul pleasures? There's nothing foul about natural desires, woma-- Priestess." Calm. He had to calm down before he pushed too far. This was a woman he couldn't afford to anger, yet the words continued to spill from his lips. "It is the natural place of a woman to know the touch of a man, they yearn for it, needing it to complete themselves." He had to find another way of expressing himself, but he couldn't stop the words now he had been given leave to speak. "You don't see it, but the women here flaunt themselves before men. They act as if they are above the men of Athens, untouchable simply because they serve in a temple. These are not sworn maidens denied the touch of man upon threat of death. No, these are normal women who would welcome the touch of a man and should do so regardless of the man who deigns to turn their way. They are not protected by honored fathers, they are single and open to the will of men." He'd said his piece. Any moment now the woman would order his chains struck free, and he would be able to find his way home.

"No, they are not. They are sworn to Hecate, beyond the reach and rule of men. Yet you would seek to force yourself upon one of the women here. You would take by force what is not offered freely to you." The woman's voice remained cold, each attack digging in beneath his skin.

"Women do not have the right to... I mean, they are the property of their family. To marry where and when their father's wish. These women, those who live here have no families."

"They serve Hecate, child. She is their mother, their father, their family.

Ophion flinched but didn't understand why. "They are women and..."

"Priestesses of Hecate; her handmaidens, in service when and where the Goddess wishes, not where a boy things they should serve, or do you believe yourself to be above the wishes of a Goddess?" Her cool gaze never left his face, eyes narrowed. "Speak the truth of your heart, boy. Hide not one detail from me."

Ophion tried to keep the words locked within, knowing the danger he would be if he spoke again. For a moment, he remained silent, but the pressure to speak became too much. "She's nothing more than another woman who has yet to learn her place. One Zeus or Ares should teach her before she infects other women with her foolishness." As the words left his mouth, he tensed. *How could I have said such a thing to her? In this place? Before Hecate herself?*

The woman nodded and turned away from him to face the statue of Hecate, her hands loose at her sides, head bowed.

He should have said something else, anything else but what had slipped free. No taking those words back and the woman, this woman, wouldn't let it go. No, he would be punished for this.

"My father will pay you as much as you desire if you agree to let me go. You know he will. No good could come from this, and no one was harmed." Her father and the money his family laid claim to had to be useful. "Unchain me, lady. And it will all be over with. Forgotten as if it has never been."

"Oh, child, you'll be unchained soon enough. When the moment is right." The Priestesslifted her arms up to the statue. "Goddess hear me and stand witness. This boy child entered your home seeking to harm those under your care. I beg of you to gift me with the means to teach this insolent pup a lesson both he and others of his kind will remember their place in this world."

The statue shimmered as the face changed, surging into life as she beautifully carved statue of the Goddess spoke.

"Foolishmale. You have dared to enter my home without permission, during a time when my children should be resting, preparing themselves for service, or serving me. Instead, you dared to place your lusts ahead of you, believing your desire to be more important than my commands. You desire their bodies and claim their service to you is a part of their lives because you were born maleinAthens."

Ophion'sthroat tightened but still the compulsion to speak what lay in his heart, took control. "They are but women, and women answer to men. Why should the women of the temple be kept above others, not bound by the rules of family and protection? This is not how things are supposed to be, as a Goddess you should know this, and not need to be reminded by a mortal."

"The beasts in the field know the female may turn away from the male if he doesn't please her. She chooses, she says who, what, and when. You are lower than any true beast, child. A monster scarred in heart and mind so your visage will reflect the heart within." The Goddess lifted her head turning toward a small opening in the roof. *"Ah, the moon will be full this time tomorrow. Fitting indeed."*

Fear clawed into the pit of his stomach. This wasn't happening. He wasn't here. He couldn't be. He was safe in his bed, with a slave girl curled up on either side of him. Maybe the spirited one from Sparta he'd taken such pleasure in breaking when she'd first been brought into the household.

Oh, how she's growled and spat at him, only to give in to being a woman when the time was right.

"Now your wicked mind focuses on monstrous desires better suited for those who lack human compassion in their souls." Hecate turned her full attention back to the kneeling Ophion. *"So it is decided. I bless you with a gift. A form to reflect the truth buried in your heart."*

"No, please..."

Light formed around the statue's fingers as Hecate lifted her hands and reached out in benediction to the kneeling Ophion. The same light moved through the air, curling and twisting its way toward him until it bathed him, covering Ophion from head to knees. Splintering torture followed on the heels of the light, tearing into him until he arched, screaming as he writhed on his knees before the Goddess.

"No!" He sobbed as he curled on his side, drawing his knees to his chest as he whimpered. Pain. Searing, burning lashing agony. Every breath hurt, nails raked their way across his lungs. He couldn't think, couldn't see, all he knew was the world of red and black torture scorching its way through his body, threatening to turn him inside out as he pleaded for mercy, swore revenge, only to beg for it to end.

Dying. He was dying. That bitch had turned the full power of her magic on him, and now it tore him apart. A slow death, a humiliating way to end his life, instead of the quick and clean way he deserved.

He twisted, trying to fight free of the light as it ate its way into him, consuming him one terrible bite at a time.

"You're not dying, boy, though you might wish otherwise when this is done. When you see your true form."

He couldn't press his hands over his ears to shut out the hateful voice of the Goddess. His muscles wouldn't obey him and the chains, still locked in place, restricted his movements.

"Kill me.... Have mercy and kill me."

"No, young one. Death would be too easy a fate for you, for everything you have done to my daughters."

He hadn't done a thing, hadn't been allowed the chance. How could she dare punish him for actions he hadn't committed?

Ophion tried to protest, but he lacked the energy for words. All he could do now was scream. He arched, back tight, heels pressed to the floor, sobbing, screaming, coughing as blood flecked his lips, only to cry again when he had the breath for it.

Then it was gone. Stripped away, leaving Ophion shaken, drenched in sweat as he laid, curled on his side on the cold, stone floor. He fought to breathe normally, but all he was capable of was submitting to the ragged gasps as they rocked through his trembling, exhausted form.

"Stand, boy," Hecate ordered.

Stand? His mind struggled with the concept as he lay

on the ice touched stone.

"*Help him, my daughter. Before the creature soils himself.*"

The Priestess moved to his side and hooked one arm beneath his left before she braced and hauled Ophion to his feet. "When the Goddess gives you an order, you obey. No matter how difficult the order may appear to be. You will rapidly come to understand how this works."

Heart pounding, throat dry, he caught the gaze of the High Priestess and looked away.

"*Your punishment is righteous, boy, and you will come to understand the full meaning of what has been done to you when the next full moon rises over the city.*"Hecate'sform wavered in front of him. The statue losing, then regaining solidity. "*Now, leave and do not enter this place, or any other which I hold domain, in this life, or the next. You and those like you are forbidden to enter any circle cast in my name. Such sacred ground will ever be denied to you.*"

He swallowed, bladder clenching. No, he wouldn't soil himself here. *Those like me?* Had she used this curse on others?

In silence, he was hauled out by two men he hadn't seen before. Warriors in Hecate's temple? When had such things been allowed?

"Argh!" He cried out as he hit the stone steps and rolled down to the damp earth below. Ribs hurt, his head pounded, and he struggled to understand the final words of the Goddess. Where their others like him, and what had she done to him?

Alena waited, the Goddess no longer present in her overpowering form, though her power lingered in soft gusts teasing dust along the marble floor. Had they done the right thing? The memory of the curse hitting Ophion's body played through her mind and doubt gnawed its way into her guts.

Cursed Blood

The Goddess was strong, powerful, the being she had dedicated her life to, yet even an immortal one could make a mistake. Had it not happened before? When Hera had cursed and tormented Hercules? The curse on Medusa? Children hidden from immortal mates, knowing their existence would trigger problems both above and below.

"If it goes wrong, if I have miscalculated, then I will correct it." Hecate's voice whispered through her mind. *"I admit to not being perfect, as I have done so before. But something had to be done if I am to protect those who are mine."*

Have faith, accept and embrace the outcome, regardless of what it might bring. "The others are adapting to the new order," she indicated the guard, unmoving against the far wall. "But I would ask, is this to be permanent, or only until the city fathers accept things need to change?"

"It is permanent. I would protect my daughters, match them with men who will protect them when need be, but never dominate them, or seek to diminish their status in my eyes."

Guards, partners, wives, husbands, and children. "Protecting your legacy, honored one?"

"Things change quickly in the mortal realm, daughter mine. If I do not act now, I may become... distracted... and lose those loyal to me when the world turns, and new ages rise."

"These changes will happen in my lifetime?" She took a deep breath to calm her now racing heart.

"No, though the first signs of the rot have begun." The goddess sighed an all too human sound. *"There are others who will come and claim this land, then a new empire, and another, and soon enough my kind will barely recognize the earth."*

"I wish I could ease your sorrows, beloved one. All I have to offer is my service, and that you will ever have." Through the darkness and light, Hecate was the center of her world, and if spilling her blood was ever needed to protect her sisters, then she would open a vein without hesitation.

"I would not ask that of you, daughter. Not when there are other services you could perform for me. Your strength, your wisdom, your courage to challenge me if you believe I go too far, these are rare qualities I would be a fool to waste."

"My wisdom is a gift which came directly from you, my Goddess." She inclined her head, only to lift it at the sound of male footsteps.

Two men, in simple tunic and sandals, with swords at their sides, entered the chamber and dropped to their knees at the edge of the circle.

"The boy?" The Priestess folded her hands in front of her body.

"Has been escorted out, lady."

Blond, with lightly tanned skin, the first man didn't match the reasonable expectations of how a man of Athens should appear, but Hecate had spoken for him, insisted this one be among the first of the guards and she was here to serve, not rule. "And word has been sent to his family?"

"Yes, lady. The messenger left as soon as word was given." Dark hair, darker eyes, the olive tone to his skin easily seen. "He is ill and is to be kept confined to the family home. No one should be permitted to visit with him from outside of the household until it can be confirmed he is not contagious."

"You've done well, return to the others and continue with your training. The temple and her people must be protected against the darkness to come." She didn't wait to see if the men would obey her, there was no need. They had come to this place willingly, called by Hecate and now their lives and their families were pledged to her service.

Families.

"Yes, daughter, you begin to understand what must be..."

CHAPTER FIVE

Ophion huddled, teeth chattering, beneath several blankets, shivering uncontrollably. Misery racked his body, his mind lost in the fog. The memory of how he'd made it through Athens to his father's villa on the outer edge of the city, was fragmented at best. Flashes of images, scents, sounds, but nothing substantial. He couldn't recall if he'd made it into his room and into his bed unaided or if a slave had supported his weight before he'd crawled beneath the blankets in the safety of his chamber.

He was safe here. Sick to his stomach, chilled and burning at the same time, but safe.

"Master, do you wish me to send for the healer?" A soft, female voice barely registered on the edge of his thoughts.

"Yes, go you, foolish girl. Go fetch the damned healer."

Ophion frowned. He hadn't spoken to the slave. Or had he? No, the order hadn't come from him. Foolish question anyway, of course, he needed to see a healer. Damned female, he'd see her punished when he recovered from whatever foul curseHecate had laid on him.

Footsteps followed and a second female voice, one he recognized this time as a woman who had been in the household for many years. "Is there anything I may do to aid him, master?"

His father? Yes the other voice, the one he'd heard, but not immediately recognized, had to belong to his father. What was he doing in his room? He never came to visit Ophion in this room. He struggled to make sense of the situation, but every time he tried to think clearly, a new wave of shivers racked his body, threatening to strip him of what focus he still laid claim to.

"When did he become ill? Quickly, girl, I must know the full tale before the healer arrives."

"Master, forgive me. I only became aware of his condition when I came to wake the young master to break his fast." The slave, Cyanea, spoke softly. Yes, it had to be the gentle, doe-eyed Cyanea, she was the one who was assigned to wake him and tend any needs he may have.

"Yet there was a message left with other slaves that he would be ill and must be kept within our walls until he recovers. How would the temple know such before you found him? And why were you not aware of this information?"

"I don't know, Master. Such wasn't shared with me."

"You should have come to me sooner, not left it until near dark to speak with me. Nor was the message shared with me until late in the day." His father snapped, one hand half lifting from his side as Ophion focused on the pair. "I should strip the flesh from your back for your laziness."

"Forgive me, please, master. I tried to find you, but none knew of your location. I swear, I searched every chamber in the villa." Cyanea bowed her head, and with his vision affected by the fever, he could see the slave trembling. "It was only when the young master's friend arrived, did anyone have a clue to your whereabouts."

"Of course Petros knew, I had business with his mother. Did you not think to question his household first?" Sharp words slapped through the air.

"No master, I'm not permitted beyond the walls--"

"Lazy piece of--"

A shadow of movement, a raised hand flashing into the air, and a cringing slave told Ophion what would happen if he didn't intervene now. "Father?" Ophion forced himself to speak. "Is it you? I cannot see you clearly." His throat ached, dry and sore. It would have been easier to swallow sand than speak, and yet he tried. "Father?"

"Ophion, my son," the larger figure moved to the side of his bed pallet. "What happened to you? What caused you to become ill? Speak to me, how could the women of Hecate know of your illness before anyone else? What happened to you?"

He wanted to tell him, speak of what had happened, but something gripped his throat, silencing him. The temple, Hecate, the curse, there had to be a way to explain it all to his father. Then he would watch the anger of the city fathers come down on the hateful women behind their marble walls.

"Ophion? Son?" A hand, large but oddly gentle, resting on his shoulder. "Do you rouse? Did I mistake a sleep and fever driven utterance for conscious speech?"

Ophion forced himself to open his eyes, he blinked and tried to focus. "Yes... I..." Speaking hurt. More than that, it was difficult, an effort to form words and he shook his head. "I wake, father."

"Bring water, bring wine. Both. Quickly girl, move." His father turned, snapping at the cowering Cyanea who darted from the room without a word. "Foolish slut, she should have woken you sooner, and now you would be in the hands of a healer, and on the road to recovery. I'll have her whipped for her laziness -- when I have the time."

The time. Yes, that was always how things worked out for his father, ever too busy to see to things to himself, Ophion had no doubt the whipping would be handed off to another. A man all too eager to earn a higher standing in the eyes of the patriarch. "No father... leave her... please. She meant... no harm."

"Why she failed in her duty, and it is important she is corrected, to set an example for the others." His father patted Ophion's shoulder. "What ails you, my son? Did you eat something foul? Drink tainted water? The wine will revive you once the foolish girl returns with it."

He couldn't speak of what had happened, couldn't tell his father of his experiences, as he tried, the pressure in his throat returned, and he was left with nothing but the ability to shake his head. Slowly the tension eased, and he closed his eyes, steadying his breathing.

Had they forbidden him to speak of the curse?

Fever, yes he could feel the fever raging through his body yet it had eased when he compared it to what he'd felt a few moments before. Was he recovering now his father had come to see him? The protection of the family? Zeus was a father, and perhaps he smiled upon those granted such care?

Yes, Zeus will protect me, and counter the curse.

"Your eyes grow clearer," his father smiled and moved his hand from Ophion's shoulder to his forehead, flicking a stray lock of hair away. "Do you feel stronger? Do you improve?"

"A little, father," Ophion admitted and tried to smile in return, but his muscles still ached. Whatever the priestess and Hecate had done to him, whatever foul spell had been used had been painful, but with Fortuna's assistance, and the blessing of Zeus, the worst had passed. "I think, with your help, I will be able to sit."

A scowl swept across his sire's face, but it was gone in a moment. "Yes, yes of course. Perhaps this is nothing more than ill humors from sleeping in too late, or from indulging in wine and richer things, but then why would they issue orders you are to be kept behind these walls until you are fully recovered?" As he spoke, the older man slid one arm behind Ophion and helped him into a sitting position, bolstering him with large cushions. "We should consult a healer or a priest. And I will demand answers from those who serveHecate. How dare they send commands to me. They have no right to order me as if I was nothing but a slave or a woman bound to their service."

Ophion wanted to protest but what would he say? He'd already found out trying to speak on what had occurred, at least to his father, was impossible. Damn them all, he wanted nothing more to do with those hateful creatures who served in temples, not after Hecate'scurse. For all, he knew the other priestesses around Athens were guilty of the same thing, but the priests? He might be safe with them.

"Petros? Is he safe?"

"He is, and he is waiting with refreshments. In time I will allow him in to see you. But not until you're stronger and I know more of what occurred last night. I would have answers, my son."

"I don't know," he protested. He did, but couldn't say it, at least not to his father. His voice sounded stronger and his vision cleared, the blurring vanished. "I don't remember much after I parted ways with Petros last night. It's hazy at best." Could he mention approaching the temple? If he couldn't, Petros would be able to.

His father paused and turned to stare at the door, gazen arrowed. "Then perhaps I should call your friend into your chamber, and we may get to the bottom of this confusing situation. If they managed to slip you a tainted draft, I would have answers then vengeance. No one strikes at my family without retribution."

Ophion nodded and lifted his hands to his temples. The pressure was still present in the back of his mind, around his chest and faint but there in his throat. The fever, though reduced, still lingered in his bones as a deep-seated ache. "It is late, is it not?" He wasn't sure, but the shadows appeared long enough to indicate it was gone noon as he glanced at the walls of his room. How long had he slept? Locked in by pain and fever.

"It will be dark before the lamps need to be trimmed, but it is already late in the day."

Moonrise. What had they said about moonrise?

"Master, I bring the wine." Cyanea returned but kept out of immediate grabbing range of his father.

Wise girl.

"Then serve it to him and be quick about it. And where is the healer?"

"Lydia runs to fetch him, master." Cyanea moved slowly to the side of the bed and offered the goblet to Ophion. "It is warmed and spiced, master. Honey for your throat."

Ophion frowned the goblet out of reach.

"Move closer to him, wretched girl." His father growled.

"Father, you're -- you're in the way. She cannot reach through you." Odd, why did he suddenly care what problems a mere slave faced in life. She was female, owned, and nothing more than replaceable property. Yet he actually cared, albeit for now, about the slave's wellbeing.

Perhaps he was sicker than he believed.

"Humph..." the older man moved away from the bed, his back stiff. "Petros, I will have him sent to you, and perhaps between the pair of you, the truth of the situation will be discovered. We will have answers before dawn, I will have it no other way."

The slave pressed the goblet into his grasp, and he drank, barely noticing when his father left the room. No doubt to hassle his mother and slaves alike, shaking anyone he could to find answers, at least until another matter captured his attention.

"Thank you, master," Cyenea murmured, and sat on the edge of the bed, one hand beneath the bottom of the goblet.

"For what?"

"Protecting me, from the Master." She inclined her head, lashes lowered, casting blue-black shadows across the upper curves of her cheeks. "It was kind of you."

Kind? No, he didn't need that reputation, not with the slaves. They would see it as a weakness and use it to their advantage. "Go, go, I'll be fine. Petros will be here shortly. Get back to your chores, girl."

Hurt flickered across her features, but she rose. "As you wish, master."

He didn't watch her leave, had no interest in making things worse by showing any care toward the slave, or the others who served the household. It was this illness, the curse, whatever Hecate had done to her, once he recovered, things would return to normal. All would make sense once he shook off the rest of it, once he was back on his feet and ready to deal with those upstart females.

"You look like shit," Petros chuckled as he entered the chamber.

"Don't feel much better," he admitted and forced himself to open his eyes. "You came to check on me."

Petros shrugged and settled down on the edge of the bed platform. "You didn't come to find me and fill me in on everything. I knew something must have happened. Now I see you, it's easy to guess Fortuna turned her face from you last night." He glanced back at the doorway and shook his head. "How much does your father know? I was told there was a message from the priestesses, the slaves are all whispering about it, much to his annoyance."

"Nothing." He'd tried, the gods alone knew he had tried. "I can't get the words out, it's like a hand grabs my throat and silences me." Ophion rubbed his throat. "It didn't go as I had hoped, I can say that much." Curses, he'd teach them about foul magic before he was done with them.

"You entered the--"

"Yes."

"This doesn't sound hopeful." Petros rubbed his temples. "Did you tangle with one of the guards? A priestess? Or worse."

"Worse." Ah, they'd let him utter single words at least, as long as he was careful.

"How so? What happened?"

"Hecate," he said. Yes, single words worked. He could work with this, for now, testing the edges of the control the women had set on him.

"The Goddess herself appeared before you?" Petros stiffened, his face drained of color. He shifted his weight, a soft tremble running through his body.

What did he have to be afraid of? Petros hadn't been in the temple. "Yes." There hadn't been any pressure on his throat, but perhaps it was because Petros had already known of his intentions, and knew where he'd been? Made sense. Why waste power on something pointless? "Punishment by Hecate."

Petros moved away from the bed, pacing several steps to put distance between them. He took a deep breath before he turned to face Ophion. "Of what sort? This fever, or is there something more, something worse to come?"

"More," he admitted, "but I don't know how bad it will be." He took a deep breath. "She said my appearance would come to match the beast within." He shivered at the retelling, remembering the way those words had lanced through his soul. What had she done to him? What curse had been laid upon him? "And I would know more, understand the curse when the full moon claimed the night. At least, I think that's what she said." Agony, too much pain to deal with, leaving his memory hazy.

"The moon grows full tonight."

The moon. No, he couldn't be here when it rose to

claim the sky. He tensed as Cyanea returned to the room and offered more wine, lifting the cup to his lips.

He pushed it away. "Not now, girl. Please. I need to think." He scowled at the female and gestured for her to move away.

"Is that all she said?"

Ophionlifted his gaze, looked at Petros and swallowed down the lump in his throat. "I need to be away from here, away from the city walls before moonrise." He didn't know what would happen to him, but he couldn't be close to his father when it happened. "Please, you have to help me before my father returns. He won't let me leave if he realizes what I'm trying to do."

"Because they sent word you were to remain behind these walls until the illness ran its course."

"It's not an illness, it's a blasted curse."

Petros shook his head, jaw set. "I can't. If--"

"You. Owe. Me."

His friend paled. "I can't, you know what will happen, your father will go to my mother, then the gates of Hades will open, and I'll never hear the end of it."

"I'll forgive the debt, every last coin if you get me out of the city." It was a lot of money to toss aside, but what other choice did he have? "Petros, you have to help me. I'm begging you."

Petros' eyes narrowed, and he walked back to the side of Ophion's bed. "You're serious about this, aren't you? You'd forgive the debt?" He paused, watching Ophion before he nodded. "Never mind, yes. I'll get you out of here." He glanced back toward the door, then at the slave girl who still lingered close to the bed, her head bowed, hair shading her features. "You, girl. Look at me."

Cynanea lifted her gaze.

"You will say nothing of this, do you understand me?"

"Yes -- Yes, masters. I understand." Cyanea nodded, her lips trembling, eyes frantic. "I will not betray you."

Despite everything, Ophion believed her.

"Priestess," the guard dropped to his knees, head bowed.

"Yes?" Alena turned, letting her gaze take in the sturdy form. Light flickered, a gentle breeze catching the flames from the lamps, sending shadows dancing across the walls.

He lifted his head, meeting her gaze. "Word has come from those set to watch the villa. The boy had visitors, from another household, and has left his home. Without the patriarch becoming aware of the situation." His voice deep, rich and tempting.

Her hands clenched at her sides, and she closed her eyes. The curse had to be confined to the villa. A place where the doors could be locked, barred, and the threshold maintained. "They were given instructions to keep the boy safe." Her jaw tight, muscles knotting with the news. "Yet they fail in the smallest tasks." Except this task wasn't small, not if the curse spread beyond the intended victims.

"Yes, Priestess."

"Is the boy being followed?" Alena turned her attention back to the waiting guard. *We can't lose him, not now. The risk is too great for the people of Athens.* And if it spread beyond the lands Athens controlled, then what? A lifetime of tracking down all those touched by the curse?

"Yes, Priestess. Two of the guards are following at a distance."

It wouldn't be enough, nor would they be safe as the guards had no skill with circle casting. "I'll assign one of the younger priestesses to this task. You will escort her to join the guards, then return to report she is safe, in place, and able to observe the events as they unfold without being spotted."

They needed to know everything that happened with the boy and his friend.

"Yes, Priestess. We are ever at your command."

Her command, Hecate'spower, in this they were one in the same. It didn't prevent the snakes knotting in her guts, or wipe away the beads of cold sweat down the length of her spine. Faith. She had to cling to her religion, her belief in Hecate and if the curse broke loose, then she and the others would serveHecate to their last breath if that's what it took to bring the spell back under control.

"Summon Fabia," Alena turned to peer over her shoulder, catching the gaze of the silent servant who stood half in the shadows. "And may Hermes quicken your steps."

CHAPTER SIX

Ophion struggled to catch his breath as Petros helped him down from the back of the horse, grunting as he did so. He bit back a groan, his limbs ached, and he knew if Petros hadn't offered assistance, he would have tumbled to the ground before they'd been halfway from the city walls. "Thank you," his voice gruff, throat sore. He swallowed, trying to get his mouth working, saliva needed but his body refused to obey him, despite all attempts to bring it to heel.

"You're looking worse than before. You had a touch color before we left, but you're green now. Are you certain this was a wise idea? I can still get us back to the city walls before the close the main gates for the night." Petros shouldered his weight and walked with him, helping him to sit on a rock before he returned to the horse, caught the reins and led the horse to a nearby, short, stubby tree, securing the animal in place.

"No. I need to stay away from the city for tonight." At least until he understood what the curse had done to him, and what he needed to do to protect his father from the fall out of Hecate's touch. "Moon should be up soon enough." He shivered. Odd, he burned one moment, froze the next. Typical for a fever, but his skin itched, crept and quivered with a mind of its own.

Petros pulled a blanket from the small pack and draped it around Ophion's shoulders. "This should help, and I'll get a fire started soon enough."

"Yes, thanks." He tugged the coarse wool around his body, fingers clinging to the cloth. "At least we'll know soon enough what that bitch has done to me."

"Don't insult her, you'll only make things worse," Petros warned.

"There's nothing more she can do to me." He sighed and scrubbed a hand over his face. Away from the city he should be safe, yet his skin crawled, the fever shifting from hot to cold and back again as he struggled to keep from curling up into a ball on the ground. "Not after everything she's already forced me to endure. I'm safe from her, for now."

"It can't be that bad. I mean, she gave you time to adapt, and maybe the punishment in the temple was the worst of it?" Petros sat the pack down and gathered the kindling needed for a fire.

No, he didn't think so but didn't speak. There'd been a coldness in the way the goddess had fixed him with her gaze, the way she had spoken. Whatever the bitch had done to him, it would be a thousand times worse than the pain he had already suffered. No, women were cruel, spiteful creatures who needed a steady hand to keep them in line.

He would provide that hand. The priestess, whatever her name was, would be among the first to pay for their crimes.

The skin across his shoulders tightened, and he lifted his head, gaze searching for a sign, for the cause of his discomfort.

"Something wrong?"

"I don't know," he couldn't be certain, but his skin itched down the length of his spine. The knowledge something was off, wrong, out of place. He rolled out his shoulders and took a deep breath. "Feel -- I feel wrong, but I don't know what it is. What's causing it." He shifted his weight on the rock and closed his eyes.

"Last part of the fever breaking, maybe?"

"I can hope, but I don't think so." No, he'd had fevers before, but it was nothing like this. "It will pass. Has to pass."

Petros set the first load of kindling down and organized his finds into piles, small items to start the fire, fuzz from dry plants, handfuls of brittle grass, seed pods. Basics needed to catch the spark from a tinder kit. At least one of them had enough sense to bring supplies. Not as if he'd had anything but wet wool stuffed inside his skull.

"Get this fire going, and you'll feel better. I brought wine, meat, cheese, bread. Dates and grapes. Should be enough to see us through tonight."

"You're a good friend, the gods themselves couldn't ask for better." He rubbed his hands over his arms, shivering despite the sweat now coating his flesh. "She'll pay for this. I'll see the priestess stripped of her rank." He coughed, chest tight, ribs sore.

"It's talking this way that got you into trouble in the first place. Might want to rethink how you're handling things." Petros struck pyrite against flint, focusing on the sparks, before leaning in and blowing on the first one to catch on the seed fuzz. "Have you warm soon enough."

Warmth wasn't the issue. Cold, hot, his body wasn't his own as long as the fever continued to control him. His muscles itched, sharp points he tried to ignore. He moaned, arms wrapped around his middle. The itch turning into something more. Pain. True torture ripped along his spine, down his legs, and into his toes. "Gods!"

"Ophion?" Petros turned, the fire forgotten. "What ails you?"

"It hurts," he groaned and slid down from the rock until he curled in a tight ball on the ground. "Thought the assault was finished, but it's back." He gulped, fighting for air. His ribs contracted, stomach rolled, sweat and pain coated his skin, and he shuddered, rocking on the ground on his side. When was it going to end? He hadn't asked for this; hadn't told him he would be forced to endure so much.

Moonrise. He needed the moon. When it rose, this end.

It had to stop. He wasn't ready for any of this and never would be.

"Make it stop," he pleaded.

"Wine, it'll help." Petros scrambled to the pack and dug through it, pulling out a skin. "Kill the senses, force you to relax. Better that than to deal with it without numbing."

Wine wouldn't help. He wasn't a fool but Petros pushed the now uncorked skin to his lips, and Ophion sipped at it. His throat half closed, yet he forced it down, the small drops of fluid easing past his fevered lips.

"Drink, you need it. Then I'll get you something to eat. Wine will ease things for you, and we can deal with the rest once you have food in you."

He shuddered, whimpering against the growing discomfort. His skin itched, burned, and he rubbed at his arms. It didn't help, but he took a sip or two of the wine before he shook his head. "I can't. No more." Tears burned in his eyes and he swallowed, forcing his throat to work again. "Need it to stop. It has to stop."

"Breath, it'll pass. You have to believe it will be over-- what the -- Zeus protect me!" Petros stumbled back from him, color stripped from his face.

Fire danced along the ends of Ophion's fingers, and he screamed, clutching them to his stomach. His vision wavered, stealing his focus, but when he pulled his hands away and tried to look at them, they weren't his own. Nails grew, thick and pointed as he stared at them, then his arms. Hair grew longer, his fingers elongated, changing in time to the throbbing searing destructive paths through his limbs and into his chest.

"Gods have mercy." Petros gasped.

"What's happening to me?" Ophion sobbed. His mouth, jaw, cheekbones, none of it felt the same. Daggers of fire touched pain stabbed into his jaw and up through his teeth. Bones cracked, nausea claiming his awareness only to fade under the endless eruptions of lancing fire. Grit pressed into his skin as he rolled, desperate to find a means of fighting the agony. He didn't deserve this, no man did, regardless of what they'd done. "I've paid the price, it needs to stop now. Should stop. I don't deserve any more of this."

"No, this isn't happening. By the Gods, this can't be real." Petros retreated. The horse reared, screaming as it bucked, and fought to be free of the reins securing it to the tree. It kicked, teeth bared, eyes rolling as it screamed again. "You're changing. This doesn't make sense. Gods. What did she do to you? Speak to me, Ophion. I can't help you if you don't tell me what to do."

Every inch of his skin now burned, stretching and changing as he struggled to understand. His teeth shifted, cracking, growing as his jaw ached, bones snapping until he screamed and rolled to his side, hugging his middle, knees drawn up. Swords of fire cut him, fire shot through him, shattering him until he howled as the last of the changes ripped their way through his helpless body.

He rolled on his back and rested, panting for breath, inhuman mouth open as he drew in air, Ophion stared up into the sky. Stones, dirt, pieces of vegetation, dug into his skin, tore at his nerves and he struggled to stay silent. For a moment his body ceased its torment, then small creaks and pops worked through his chest, ribs resettling into place as he continued to adapt. The sky didn't appear the same. He frowned. What was going on? The stars were brighter, and there were more of them. A hundred scents assaulted his nostrils carried by a soft breeze now teasing at his fur.

Fur?

Yes, the hair on his arms, the backs of his hands, his face, it had all changed.

Slowly, his limbs no longer his own, he shifted to his

stomach and pushed to his feet. Rags clung to his body, and he clawed them aside, tossing the remains to the dirt before he stared at his hands.

No, claws. Long fingered claws covered in a luxurious, dark fur. His mouth dried out. He tried to lick his lips, but a long, bestial tongue swiped out over teeth which had become sharp dangerous fangs. He shook his head, attempting to resettle his vision, but what he saw, how he had changed, wasn't about to vanish.

"What happened to you?" A voice. One he knew.

Petros? Yes, it had to be. Petros had come with him, been at his side when this had begun. Who else would it be but the only man he could indeed call a friend.

He shifted his weight, searching for the source before his gaze narrowed on the man and the horse he struggled to control. The large animal bucked, kicked and whinnied, its distress filling the air, tempting him to draw closer. He sniffed the air, tasting it. Meat. Fresh meat. Blood pounding through delicate flesh. The scent combined with fear, sweat, uncertainty, and called to him.

He swallowed, his mouth now filled with saliva, his stomach growling with the need to bite, rip, shred the offering before him and fill his belly with the rich, warm food.

No, he couldn't think this way. The horse wasn't food. Petros wasn't a meal.

Meat. Blood. I need to eat.

He shook his head, trying to shake off the need to leap at the horse, attack it, pull the creature to the ground and dig his new, sharp claws into the quivering flesh. Petros. The horse. Either would do. He needed food. Needed their blood.

Kill them.

"Ophion?" Petros had one hand on the horse as he spoke. "Answer me, please, or I must leave. I-- I can't stay if you don't answer me. I need to know you're still in there. Oh,

Gods, please still be in there."

Ophionlifted his head and growled the single word. "Run."

"What?" Petros moved, a half step back. "Ophion, can you understand me?" He pulled himself on the back of the terrified horse.

"Run!" He growled, baring his teeth. Fear hung heavy in the air, calling to him. "Now." He crouched, claws spread, ready to move, to pounce and claim his prey.

Petros dug his heels into the flanks of the horse, and it was all the encouragement the animal needed. The horse, now freed from the reins, bolted and tore across the ground, away from Ophion. Sweat lathered the mount as it tried to flee.

Mine!

Ophiongrowled and started after them. His new, longer, more powerful legs, helped him eat up the distance between Ophion and his prey. He reached out with his claws. *Claws, I have real claws.* Weapons he could use against either an enemy or to bring down his food.

All he needed was a few more steps, and he'd be on him.

He swept out one hand, the tips of his claw catching and raking lines along the flank of the fearful creature.

"No!" Petros screamed, trying to urge the horse into a faster pace, heels slamming against its flanks. "Ophion, don't do this."

Too late. His claws dug fully into the side of the terrified animal, bringing it down against the ground with a powerful tug sent both rider and horse sprawling across the field. He laughed, howling in delight before Ophion bent and sank his teeth into the throat of the screaming horse.

"No. Oh, Gods, Ophion, please." Petros cried out.

Blood. Hot, fresh blood poured into his mouth. He lifted his head and swallowed it down. Life. Pure, powerful, life rich liquid filled his mouth again when he reclaimed the dying animal's throat. He laughed, his delight carried by growls of pleasure and he drank, tasting the intoxicating mix of fear, pain, and energy swamping his taste buds, filling his stomach as he gulped and chewed on heated flesh.

"Don't make me do this, Ophion. You're my friend, I don't want to hurt you. I've never wanted to harm you." Petros pleaded his voice near.

Ophion didn't care, why would he? Petros was human, weak, he couldn't harm him. He tore another chunk from the horse, swallowing it now without chewing. More. He needed more.

"May the Gods forgive me for what I must do."

The hairs on the back of Ophion's neck rose as he turned, eyes narrowed. A sword glinted in Petros' hand. Ophion acted before he had time to think it through. He lashed out at his friend, knocking the man aside. "I told you to run." He snarled at his one-time friend, all too aware of the blood now dripping from his mouth, jaw, and teeth.

Petros stumbled back, one hand on his abdomen.

The delicious aroma from the horse, the pull of meat, drew Ophion's attention back to his waiting meal. He would deal with Petros later, once he'd eaten his fill. Nothing else mattered beyond the horseflesh he could now fill his stomach with.

Even the subtle, tempting smell of his friend's blood wasn't enough to pull him away from the welcoming, hot, salt heavy, blood-drenched horseflesh waiting for him.

CHAPTER SEVEN

Ophion'sstomach groaned as he crawled to the remains of the fire Petros had attempted to start. Full, stuffed beyond reason, the meat lay heavy in his belly. He'd overeaten in a body he barely recognized, he knew the cause. He rolled to his back and tried to stretch out, hoping it would help.

It didn't.

"What have you done?"

He knew the voice. Connected it with his friend, the man who had tried to help him, but didn't care.

"Ophion?" The single word a moan of misery.

"Be. Silent." He growled, not wanting to be disturbed. Sleep. As a hunter, he needed to rest and allow his body the chance to digest his meal.

"You -- you attacked me."

Ophion closed his eyes to shut out the noise.

Cold and wet something dropped on the end of his nose. Another on his cheek. He blinked and opened his eyes as he registered the droplets of water striking his naked flesh.

Rain.

What in the name of Hades was he doing out where he could be rained on? Had he fallen asleep in the courtyard of the villa? No, not possible, he wouldn't have been left out here naked. One of the slaves would have woken him, or at least thrown a blanket over him.

He stretched and winced, biting back a groan. Aches claimed his limbs, his bones burned and something stuck to his flesh. His other senses struggled to life. Where was his bed? The slaves? His room? He blinked and tried to clear his vision, but his eyes were slow to respond.

Outside.

He twisted, searching for familiar locations and land-marks. Beyond the city walls, it was the only thing which made sense. This wasn't within the walls of Athens, nor close enough to see the walls from his current location. And he was -- naked?

Ophiongrowled and rolled to his feet, glancing down at his naked form. No, not entirely nude, not if he counted the dried blood coating his skin.

A horse, or the remains of one, lay a distance away. Clawed open, blood staining the ground, flies buzzing at the wounds and spilled entrails. He stumbled toward it. Had he ridden out here?

A low whimper, human, pain-filled, drew his atten-tion.

"Who's there?"

"Ophion?" Weak but familiar the voice called out.

"Petros?" He stumbled toward the voice, searching the ground. Was his friend injured? Had he been hurt? No, the blood wasn't his. "Are you alright?"

"Hurt," Petros admitted.

Ophionpaused, trying to locate the source of the voice. "Where are you?"

"This way. Gods, you hurt me, Ophion. Really hurt me this time."

How in the name of Hades had he ever managed to harm his friend? "I don't remember."

Petros coughed, the sound wet and worrying, but it was enough to encourage Ophion to hurry. He followed a small path around a large outcrop of rocks and stopped. Pet-ros lay on the ground, curled on his side, blood marking his chest, the tunic, and the dirt around him.

"What happened?"

"You," he coughed and tried to sit up.

"Wait, I'll help you." Ophion moved behind him, helping Petros into a seated position. "I did this to you? How's that possible?" He reached for Petros' hand and moved it away from the injury. Four deep gashes marked Petros' chest. Claw marks? But what type of animal could cause this type of injury? "I couldn't have done this to you, or anyone else." He pressed his friends' hand back over Petros' chest.

"You changed, last night. Into something else. A beast. Claws. Teeth. Fur." Petros shook his head. "You were ill, remember? Cursed by Hecate."

Ophion withdrew his hand and shook his head. It wasn't possible. Yet he'd been cursed. Pain. A fever. Petros had helped him escape the villa, break free of the confines of Athens walls. "No, I wouldn't have done this to you, even if it were possible." Images, blurred at first, claws bursting from his fingers, heavy fur covering his flesh, the back of his hands, his arms. Teeth, they'd changed, his jaw breaking to adjust to the new fangs. Yes, fangs, teeth was too tame a word to use for what had filled his mouth. "Hecate cursed me, yes, I remember some of it." What else had he forgotten?

"Yes, for trying to enter the temple and use one of the women for your pleasure. I told you not to go. Now, look at me," Petros whimpered and glanced down at his chest. "I'm going to die, aren't I?"

"Maybe. I don't know how bad it is." The scent of blood filled the air, coated his flesh, and now he was faced with the possible death of his best friend. "I can take another peek, then find water or wine to wash the wounds. Wine would be better."

"I have some with the pack," Petros inclined his head in the direction of the steaming pile of horse remains. "It wasn't on the horse when I tried to leave last night. I'd given you a drink, which means it would be by the fire." He coughed, blood flecking his lips. "Not supposed to cough blood." He leaned down and closed his eyes. "I'll be right here, waiting."

Ophion cringed. No, his friend wasn't going any-where, not until the bleeding was under control. Hecate. Blasted bitch. The woman was dangerous, Goddess or not, and would pay for her crimes.

He hurried away, wincing at the remains of the horse. Had he done the damage to the horse and his friend? No, he didn't want to think about it. His fingers flexed, the tips of his fingers aching with the need to do act. Dive into the re-mains of the horse and what? Feed? His stomach growled at the idea. How was it possible, if he'd eaten earlier, hadn't he?

A flash of memory. Rich, moist meat, horseflesh, and blood filling his mouth.

Delicious.

The horse. Gods, he'd killed and eaten the horse. Would he do the same to Petros?

Of course not. He's my friend.

It hadn't stopped him from attacking his friend last night.

He snatched up the pack and the wineskin and rubbed at his arms. His skin itched from the dried blood. A stream, there'd be one close enough, he could wash himself off once he'd seen to Petros. Then what?

"Hot," Petros whined. "Cold. Hurts."

"Fever?" Ophion dropped to his knees and reached out, brushing his fingers over Petros' forehead only to yank his hand back. "Burning up." Like he had. Could it be Hecate had cursed both of them? Or was he responsible for it? He stared at his hands, the dried blood beneath his claws. "What have I done to you?"

CHAPTER EIGHT

"Lady, it is done." Fabia eased to her knees in front of Alena. "But I have foul news."

Alena turned, arching an eyebrow as she let her gaze rest on the younger woman. "Tell me."

"He marked his friend, and the curse has been passed on beyond the safety of villa walls. The one named Petros now carries the mark of the beast, and the cursed one has realized he can share the curse with others. The idea, for now, horrifies him."

The curse had to be contained. "Are they still in the same place? Or have they returned to Athens?" If they had returned behind the city walls but free to roam, the two men would be able to infect the entire populace. Yet outside they might spread the beast through the whole world.

"They remain at their camp. Petros is injured, and the fever builds in him. He will change come moonrise." Fabia pushed back her shoulders, her voice calm. "We could take them now, Lady. Though once the moon shows her face, Ophion will be stronger and more difficult to dispose of."

"Describe what you witnessed, how Ophion appeared when in the throes of the curse."

"Tall. His shoulders are wide, back curved, so the back and neck appeared to be one from behind." Fabia paused, brow furrowed as she continued. "Fur, a mix of brown and black. Still male, his parts are easily seen. Fur on his face, his jaw a mix of wolf and human, fangs in place of teeth. His eyes glow, yellow, but sick with a touch of green. Ears, like a wolf's, same with his tongue. Yet he lacks the beauty of such creatures. Claws where hands and fingers should be, sharp, dangerous. His voice a growl, but understandable if he speaks with care to be understood. His legs are strong, thighs big, but his calves, lower legs, shaped more like the Minotaur, but with claw-tipped paws instead of hooves."

Alana closed her eyes and allowed the image to form in her mind. Beast, monster, she shuddered at the idea but didn't let her fear to take control of her. No, she was bound to Hecate. Would never turn her back on her Goddess, no matter if she remained fearful of what the curse had brought about. "Then we have much to do. Gather the guards. And those of our number who are skilled with slingshot and dagger. Our guards will need the support from our sisters and daughters." And she would need the aid of Hecate to survive what was to come.

"As you wish, Lady."

"You will always have my support, daughter mine. You and all those sworn to my service. Take with you the items needed to create a circle. Casting such may be your final weapon." The voice of the Goddess echoed through the chamber. *"It is time we protect Athens."*

"Petros, look at me," Ophionlifted the second skin to his lips. "You need to drink. It will help."

Petros moaned and shook his head. "No, I need to die. I don't want to become the same thing you've become. Sorry old friend." He coughed, blood marking his lips once more. "Let me go, Ophion. Let me die, or better yet, help me die."

"No, not happening." Ophion snapped and pushed the skin to Petros' mouth. "Drink. You're not going to leave me like this. Not on my own." If he'd been cursed, he'd be better off with a friend at her side. "Listen to me, we can go to the temple and get them to cure us. They cursed me, not you. The goddess will help you regardless if she refuses to do the same with me."

Petros turned his head away. "It won't work. I'll be

like you. I'll be locked out from my home."

"From a mother who treats you like a child, you mean? Besides, you don't know if it will work or not. We have to try. I don't care if they kill me, or leave me to die in a cell, as long as they help you." *Why does it matter if he's healed? I won't be on my own if he becomes like me. We can explore the world together, strong enough to never have to face danger again. Not without being able to destroy it.* Yes, he liked the idea. Petros with him, fighting by his side. Finding the right females to tumble.

His friend cried out, a wave of fresh agony striking the man as he writhed on the ground.

Nothing he could do but wait until the moon rose, if he were lucky Petros would survive. He'd no longer be alone in life, this new cursed life he had been locked into. And if he could turn one person, perhaps he could do the same with others. His father, for instance.

The idea bubbled away in the back of his mind. Yes, the more of his kind existed, the better it would be, but not yet. Not until he understood the strengths and weaknesses of his new form. Plans formed, the knowledge he had much to learn about turning into the beast. As the day passed, more pieces of information, images of what he had done through the night, returned to him. He'd had control, of sorts. Not attempted to eat Petros, only the horse.

If I was indeed a monster, I'd have eaten Petros, savaged him. I didn't. I tossed him aside.

Injured him, but only in separating Petros from his chosen meal.

"Kill me, please. Ophion, I'm begging you, end it for me." Petros weakened voice drew his attention. "If you have any care for me, take my dagger and cut my throat."

Ophion sighed and glanced at the weapon he'd stripped away from his companion earlier in the day. "No, I'm not going to kill you. I've offered to take you into the city, remember? They will be able to cure you." He settled down by Petros, and reached out, smoothing one hand over his friend's sweat-damp hair. "But I won't kill you." The bitches in service to Hecate might.

After all, why cure a man you'd cursed in the first place?

They didn't curse Petros. Or maybe they did, through me, because he was involved in the plan?

Gods, it would be like those foul females, lashing out at decent men for no other reason than they could. Regardless of what plans he'd drawn Petros into, the man hadn't done a damn thing to those in the temple. In fact, he'd pleaded with Ophion to change his mind. If anything, Petros should be one of the ones protected from the curse.

"Give me my dagger."

"No, my friend. Not today." Not ever if he had his way, but by tomorrow Petros might be dead. If he weren't, then he'd be changed, cursed, but stronger, faster, able to hunt to fight in ways he'd never had the chance to before today. "When you're strong again, we'll return to the city, seek out healers. You'll be yourself once more." Or a new version of the man he called a friend.

A sound, low, barely audible, drew his attention. A noise he might not have caught, or acknowledged, before last night. He lifted his head and inhaled.

Men. No, men and women. At least one, woman, perhaps two?

Odd, he shouldn't be able to tell gender from here, when he couldn't see them. Yet his nose said people, told him their sexes and gave him a rough idea of number and direction due to the differences in aromas with each person. Six, four men, two women.

A scent of oil lingered with the men. Weapons? He couldn't tell from this distance.

"We're not alone," he leaned in over Petros. "Stay here, I need to find out what they're doing here and if they've come to help."

"Give me my dagger," Petros demanded.

"No, you'll use it on yourself." He pressed one hand on his friend's shoulder, pressing him back to the earth. "Don't move, you'll open up the wounds." He glanced at the injury. No, he wasn't seeing things, Petros was healing. Slow but still faster than he should be.

The curse?

What else could it be? Perhaps another god had taken a hand in the situation.

Ares, my loyalty has ever been with you.

Would the god of war accept him in his new form? He couldn't see why not, wasn't he a better warrior in his new form? One able to embrace all war had to offer? A problem he would confront at a later date when he next made an offering to Ares.

He edged toward the newcomers, keeping low to the ground, naked and unashamed. If the women hadn't wanted to see a nude man, they shouldn't have come out here, away from the safety of their home.

He frowned, how did he know where they had come from?

The scent, a hint of the incense he associated with temples?

"Come no closer, Ophion." A man's voice, strong, confident and commanding.

"Who are you to give me orders?" Ophion snarled, his jaw aching. It wasn't moonrise, yet he could feel the beast beneath his skin. "I don't know you."

"We know you, cursed one. The GoddessHecatetouched you, and we are here in her name." The man continued. "You will surrender to us, be bound, and be brought before the High Priestess for judgment."

Ophion laughed, his muscles knotting, toes curling into the dirt beneath his feet. "Judgment? She passed her hateful curse on me. Now you think I would willingly kneel before that bitch again?" He lifted his head and stared at the sky. "You hear me, Hecate? I will not come to you, not for my sake." Nor for his friend, not if it meant doing it as a prisoner, shamed and bound for all to see. No, he wasn't a slave to be dragged through the city or a criminal.

A woman gasped, her sound soft and tempting. His body hardened at the sound of the female, the need to claim one, to feel soft flesh beneath him, rose, demanding attention. Yes, he'd keep one of the priestesses when this was done, perhaps change her, let the curse take her the same way it had with Petros. They would need females, but would it be better to mark them, or leave them as untouched? Was it possible?

These were things he could deal with later.

"You will bring down Hecate's wrath." The man warned.

"And what would you call this curse?" Ophion laughed. Didn't they understand what he'd been put through? How he'd changed? "There's nothing more she can do to me unless she kills me, and perhaps I'd welcome death?" He took another step toward them, letting his new senses take in the changes in the area. Small sounds of mice and other rodents scurrying to hide. The lighter steps of the women. Oil, herbs, and salt?

Why would they bring salt?

It wasn't long until moonrise, and he'd be able to fight them in his full new form. Then what would they do? He felt stronger than he had before. Yes, he was naked, unarmed, but they feared him, feared Petros or they would have attacked by now. Done everything they could to bring the two men under their control.

Yet they hadn't moved.

"You could beg her forgiveness if you surrendered to us. Then she might ease the fate of your friend." The stranger suggested.

"But not me, right? No, the bitch has done her worst to me, and I am to continue to suffer. Ah, but did she know at the time I could turn others? Pass on the curse? I don't believe she thought that one through, do you?"

"Your family failed in their duty. They were to keep you locked in the villa." A second voice, female, answered. "They should have watched you, the way they were told to. Now we must clean up their mess."

He growled. The bitch had sent him to infect his family. Would all of them have died, or been put in cages, a means of teaching families and the council the error of their ways when it came to their sons? His family hadn't deserved such treatment. "I would have harmed them."

"Perhaps, or they might have found safety in their rooms, perhaps behind strong doors." A cold, clear reply from the priestess.

Bitch, she's no better than the rest of them. They'd pay, every one of them would pay. He stared down at his hands, still human but for a small glint at the end of his nails. Stronger, thicker than before, not full claws, but enough he could use them to lash out, and he could feel the change approaching, slow and smooth as the night drew in.

Would it only happen during the full moon, or would he learn to use his gifts at other times?

"Will you surrender yourself?"

"No!" He growled, spit frothing on his lips. His jaw burned with the need for his fangs to replace teeth. "I will not give myself into the care of those females." How could they believe he would surrender, welcome the protection of the women who had cursed him, touched him with this stronger form, the power which surged through his body, willing him to reach for it.

Could I do it before the moon rises?

Tempting, but he didn't need the full strength of the beast, the creature lurking beneath the surface of his otherwise human skin.

"You would defy a Goddess?" The woman asked.

"I am made a God, I need no Goddess, answer to none. I am Ares creature now." War, chaos, death, blood, these were the forces he would give himself to, not a Goddess who would see him captured, neutered, unable to turn others, forbidden to ever bring another into the grace he now claimed as his own. No, a mistake he would never make, regardless of which Goddess tried to call him to his knees.

Softer voices, a conversation he wasn't meant to hear, but his new skills allowed him to follow every word.

"We can't leave them here, they'll infect others and unleash a plague." A second woman, the one who had not spoken before. "Her orders were clear, we bring them in. One way or another."

"Agreed, if Ophion has not yet learned his lesson in obedience, then we must bring him to Hecate regardless of his wishes." A man, the one who had called out originally.

"It will not be easy, but with the blessing of the Goddess, we will complete the task."

He laughed, the sound guttural, powerful and dangerous. His claws grew, pushing out from beneath his nails. It should have hurt, it did, but the small stinging pain nothing compared to what he had already endured during his first turn, his original introduction to the curse now burning through his blood.

"Ophion," Petros groaned, his voice agony filled and distant. "Go with them. I would know the blessing of the Goddess before I die."

"Your friend speaks sense." The second woman.

"He is in great discomfort, the curse surges through his body, preparing him. Once he survives the first turn, he will understand this is a blessing. What your bitch would turn into death, my death is but a new source of life, power, strength." He could control Athens itself, once he had enough people turned, enough men. Even if he touched women with his gift, they would be proper females, ones who knew their place.

"He will die, he won't survive the turning." A male voice, not one who had spoken before. Doubt clung to the man's voice.

"Is that what one of the priestesses told you? If it was true, why would you be out here, worried I'll make others like me? Why would she send you out here?" He edged closer, steps silent. Odd, he'd never been a hunter, yet now his body adapted to the quiet he needed to use, the steps of a tracker or predator following prey.

"To offer you mercy." The man insisted.

Ophion didn't answer but crouched down, his feet changing, toes lengthened, claws tipping them, hair thickening until it covered most of his lower leg. Moonrise, it drew closer, he could feel it, sense it, a tingling awareness across his skin and into his soul.

A smile split his features. They would pay.

CHAPTER NINE

"Where is he? Where is my son? And the boy, Petros? Get the High Priestess, she is behind this. I demand she show herself!" The voice carried through into the depths of the temple. "I will have answers."

No wonder Ophion showed no respect for Hecate if this was the way his father behaved. Alena cast a glance at the silent statue of Hecate and took a deep breath. She might be a woman, one he was used to being able to command, but in this place, she was the one who ruled, in Hecate's name, not him.

"Lady, should I have the guards escort him out?" A servant bowed her head.

"No, but have them at the ready in case I need assistance." Alena kept her voice calm and steady. "If he proves as foolish as his son, then he will come to understand how things work." Hecate preserve her. How many other men or families would turn away from the respect due to the gods? "I will attend him shortly."

She smoothed her hands down her robes, glancing at the back of them. Wrinkles, the first small brown spots marking age, nails kept short, with one finger curved more than the others, the flesh memory of a broken bone many years ago. She was growing old, soon it would be time to choose the one who would replace her, begin the final training and step back into the shadows to enjoy her last years in Hecate'scare.

Goddess forgive me if I lose my temper with this foolish mortal. He knows not the risks he takes by storming into your temple. She sent the silent prayer out into the world and counted, eyes closed, to one hundred before taking a single step.

Lamps and torches flickered in the wake of her slow,

calm passage through the corridors, robes whispering over stone floors as she made her way through from the private rooms, areas few not in service to Hecate would ever see. Head held high, hair now touched with silver, half covered by a light veil pulled back from her head when she moved.

Alena paused behind the door and listened.

"How dare she keep me waiting."

"The lady will be here when her time permits," a soft, gentle voice.

"Do not think to speak to me, unless I ask you a direct question, woman." A snarled response.

Ah yes, the city fathers needed to be reminded of their service to the gods. Did they treat those who served Athena the same way? Perhaps it was why the city had suffered such strife in her lifetime, with raids, illnesses, and loss of trade in the past few years. The people cried out to the gods for aid, yet those who led the city turned their backs on the gods they demanded help them, protect them.

She sighed.

The world changed, faster than she was happy with, but wasn't that the nature of the old, or middle-aged? Change was for the young, those with minds flexible enough to adapt. Not men and women stuck in their ways.

"Foolish female, if she believes she has the upper hand in keeping me here. She only makes matters worse. I will have answers. I will have things corrected, and if she doesn't appear soon, I will search for her and drag the woman out here to answer on her knees.

A hiss of shock, but the woman waiting with Ophion's father, remained silent other than the small outburst.

Good, she understands saying anything will only add to his rage. She glanced at the waiting warriors and inclined her head. Anger flitted across their features, the need to burst in and deal with the ignorant man. If he attempted anything, she knew the guards would come to her aid, if she required it.

With silent dignity, she nodded for one of them to open the door and walked through into the main public chamber.

"About time, where in Hades where you?" He turned, eyes narrowed. Small lines furrowed his brow. Eyes dark and sullen, hair thinning with traces of grey, but broad-shouldered and the trace of muscles, tone which had come from a harder life than she would have expected from a man with his wealth. "I will have answers in regards to my son and his friend."

She didn't answer, but folded her hands in front of her, head up, back straight, features schooled, she hoped, into a mask of calm as she watched the new arrival.

"Have you nothing to say?" He stalked toward her.

Alena didn't move, didn't back down. "When you remember where you are, and who rules here, then we will talk. However, if you continue to act as if you are a child, unschooled in the ways of the Gods, then we will wait. The choice is yours, Daichi."

He blanched but didn't back down. "You are a woman in Athens, a city where men rule. This is not the Amazon tribe, nor Sparta. We know how to keep our females in line here, and you will answer me."

Alena bit back a sigh. There would always be those who refused to learn. "Then I will leave, and have you escorted out."

"You can't dismiss me as if I were nothing more than a slave. You need to answer me. I will have information about my son before I leave." He stalked toward her.

Alena raised a hand, preventing the guards from stepping in. "Do you really believe you will be allowed to touch me, Daichi?"

"I'm not afraid of your pathetic Goddess."

The wind whipped its way through the chamber,

circling the men and women before it focused on Daichi. It howled and attacked him, knocking him to the floor. He turned, struggling to get to his feet. But the wind continued to assault him. Lashing the man from one side of the room to the other. Letting up only for a few seconds before it began again, turning him this way and that as he screamed in rage, protesting before the sounds turned to uncertainty than fear.

Alena didn't move, the wind barely touching her.

"Enough!" Daichi commanded.

The wind paused, then struck him full in the chest, pushing him back against the far wall before it lifted him, pummeling him with unseen blows. Did he genuinely believe he had the power to command a Goddess? Alena smiled as she watched, then forced her features back into the much-needed mask of calm confidence.

"Lady?" One of the younger servants leaned close, her voice pitched low.

"We will wait, young one. He will learn his lesson soon enough." She let her gaze shift to the servant and reached out, touching the girl on the shoulder. "You are safe here, under the protection of Hecate." Beyond the temple was another situation, but she wasn't about to remind the maiden of such things. "The guards are also close at hand, and he has no power here, never will. He will learn, or he will be removed from these sacred grounds."

"Yes, lady."

Once, when the Gods had been appropriately revered, the man would have been executed for his actions. Those days where the Gods and Goddesses had been honored, were long gone and unlikely to return in her lifetime, if ever. Other Gods threatened from distant lands, some seeking to exist alongside those who claimed Athens, Sparta and the rest of Greece, then there were the ones who believed the only way to survive was to destroy everything in their path and force the mortals left behind to bend the knee.

"Enough, please." Daichi pleaded.

The wind ignored him, knocking the man from one end of the chamber to the other three times before it dumped him at Alena's feet. She peered down at the shuddering figure as he lay on his back on the stone floor. She said nothing, offered no aid. He'd been punished by Hecate, and she would show him no mercy, no relief.

The man rolled to his stomach and moved slowly to his knees, panting for breath, gulping in air. "You had... had no right."

Alena sighed. "What happened to you was not my doing, Daichi."

"You claim this was your goddess?" He stood.

"Stay on your knees," she gestured to where he knelt. "Unless you wish to give the impression you require another lesson from Hecate?"

"Arrogant bitch, like your so-called damned Goddess."

The wind returned. Loud. Angry. It snapped across his face with the sound of a slap. His head snapped to the side. He took a breath and returned his gaze to Alena, a thin trickle of blood spilled down from the corner of his mouth.

"It is best you remember where you are." Alena forced herself to remain calm. "I am not behind the attack on you, but Hecate is. If you would leave here alive, you would be better off begging for her forgiveness before we tend to any other matters."

Daichi bared his teeth in a silent snarl.

If she had to wait, she would do it. Patience was one of the many skills she'd had to learn through the years. Service demanded patience, the ability to remain calm, her hands clasped before her body. A short time, an afternoon, all day and into the next, she was capable of waiting for as long as required.

"Are you done?" She raised an eyebrow and watched him, waiting for a time when he would make a decision and speak once more. "Or should I ask Hecate if she wishes to continue your education?" For once she permitted a soft smile to claim her lips. So, perhaps, she had a wicked streak in her, even if she only allowed it out to play from time to time.

"Where is my son?" He demanded, though his voice shook.

She sighed and rolled her eyes. Whatever she did, it wasn't going to change his focus. "Your son tried to defile maidens sworn unto Hecate and has paid the price. Be thankful his punishment didn't include you or your family." It should have done, but the love of a friend had changed matters. Did Ophion deserve the loyalty and friendship offered by Petros? No, not if his actions before and since the visit to the temple were anything to go by.

"Why would my family be punished for the actions of one member?"

"Your only son. A child who hadn't been raised to respect the Gods and those who serve them." She arched an eyebrow. "It would be best if you remember his actions reflect upon you and your family." No, why would he think of such things? "Your son was punished, what happens from this point out depends on his actions, and yours." She met his gaze, eyes narrowed, voice calm. "Do you understand, Daichi?"

"Punished how?" He ground his teeth.

"His outer self shall reflect his inner beast, preventing others from ever forgetting who he truly is." She repeated a version of the words Hecate had shared with Ophion. "He is marked and will remain this way unless the Goddess offers him a cure." Not entirely a lie. Death would free Ophion of the curse, as it needed a living body to exist or be passed on to another.

"She cursed my son?"

"Yes, with cause. Would you question the will of the gods?"

He growled and looked away. No matter what his instincts demanded, at least the man appeared to have learned verbally assaulting Hecate in her own home was a fool's game. "No, I honor her wishes."

And begrudge the limitations it enforced on his behavior. She inclined her head. "At this point, your son and his friends are beyond the city walls and offer a threat to us if they are not contained. It would appear Ophion was unable to control himself and attacked his friend, and now there are two who are touched by the curse and must be brought to heel."

Daichi's brow furrowed, eyes narrowed. "You plan on killing him."

"Not I, Daichi. What Hecate had plans, is up to the Goddess, but I will say this much. The risk your son poses, thanks to disobeying orders given to your household to keep him secured behind walls, is real and members of the temple are currently attempting to contain him." How much more should she tell the man? *Nothing, he's dangerous. Almost as much as his son.* "You will not interfere with the affairs of Hecate but will return to your home and tend to your household. Perhaps you will be fortunate enough to have another child, but count this one as dead, in the hands of the Gods. Mourn him, follow through with your rites, and go on with your lives."

"What? No, he still lives, he will continue to live." Daichi protested and rose, forgetting his position on the floor. "Outside of the walls, fine. I'll find him. I won't let you kill my son. Not for being a young man, for following through on his desires."

"Desires are one thing, attempting them is another.

One we will not forgive. And if you can't remember your place is on your knees here, then it is best you leave." She didn't move, didn't wait to see what Daichi would do. "Now."

Daichi's eyes narrowed, his voice cold. "This isn't over, woman. Not for you or your goddess." He turned, head held high as he stalked out of the chamber.

"No, I don't suppose it is."

Claws bit into flesh, and he howled in delight. Blood and pieces of human male scattered from his blow as he turned, searching for the next target. One man stood next to a young woman. No, not next to, behind.

Coward. He thinks the woman won't be harmed. Ophion smiled, exposing his teeth at the couple, nose twitching. A scent, one he hadn't expected, hit him and he took a step forward. Salt. Why would they have salt here? He tipped his head, taking in the pair. A trap? No, he didn't scent others, only the men and women he'd located originally.

A moan of pain filtered through his concentration. Not Petros. The one he'd struck, torn into and knocked to the earth. Blood spilling to the eager, hungry dirt.

"Cease your attack, Ophion." The man commanded.

"Make me," he laughed, lifting his head, drinking in the slow change of the sky. Night would come, the moon's light to guide him, but he didn't need it to see his prey. "You're weak. Foolish. Think I will not attack a woman? Oh, I will. She serves Hecate; she's prey to me." He took a step toward them, but they didn't move, didn't back away. His eyes narrowed, what made them confident they could stand against him?

The scent of salt grew as he approached, his gaze scanning the ground. Salt on the ground. Around the two of them. He inhaled, taking it in, not understanding what was going on. Salt. He leaned in, tasting the scent, and more. A crackle of energy. Why would they spread a circle of...

Circle?

Magic? A spell?

He snarled and backed up. "What is this?" He gestured at the circle.

"This is a power you can't cross." The woman explained, her voice calm, chin raised. "There are powers in this world which all must obey. A circle of protection, filled with Hecate'spower." No bragging, or pride, only words. Simple words.

No, he wasn't weak. Wouldn't be kept out by a line of salt. He snarled at the couple, then stopped. The other two, he'd lost track of them.

Something struck his back. Fire erupted, and he turned, reaching for the point between his shoulder blades. The spear moved as he attempted to pull it free, but he couldn't reach it, couldn't grasp the shaft and turned, growling in growing frustration.

A warrior from the temple stood with the other woman behind him, her lips moving, but whatever she said, he couldn't hear. He stalked toward the man, growling his anger, agony, and frustration at the male. Death. The man would pay for what he'd done. Then he would deal with the rest. The women, the remaining male, they'd know the danger of attacking him.

"You can't harm us, beast." The second woman, younger, barely more than a child, spoke. Her voice stronger than her years. "You will submit to the will of Hecate, or you will die here, with no family to mourn your loss. But your death will not be the only one. Your friend will die out here, alone, and forgotten because of your pride. All you had to do was bow before Hecate, accept your fate, and all would have been as it should be. Instead, you tainted your friend, your only friend."

Ophion glanced back in the direction of Petros. No, he had more than one friend, no matter what they believed. Petros was the one he was the closest to. "I will keep him safe."

"It's too late for that, you made a mistake by passing on the curse."

No, it hadn't been a mistake. He growled and stalked toward the couple. No woman had the right to speak to him like this. Not a priestess of Hecate, or the goddess herself. "I will show you." He tried to ignore the lance of fire in his back. It would be dealt with soon enough, once he had everything under control when the men were dead and the women subdued, bound to his will.

Changed. Yes, he'd turn them when he was confident they were obedient.

Magic flared as he charged at the two. Except... only one of the pair hid within a circle of salt. Not the man. He smiled, growling as he attacked. The man lifted his shield, half crouching, the leaf shaped blade in hand. His spear already spent between Ophion's shoulders.

It wouldn't be enough.

He growled, launching himself at the lone man. The others behind him, those in their pathetic salt protection, would be next. It might stop him, but would it stop a weapon? A spear, rock, sword? He'd find out soon enough, then they would all pay for their crimes.

His heart raced, teeth bared as he stalked toward the waiting male. He'd die first.

"Surrender." The warrior demanded.

Ophion didn't respond. He growled and launched himself at the male. Words no longer needed.

"In Hecate's name, I command you to halt." The woman's voice rang out, power behind her words, but she remained in the circle.

The sword lashed out, metal biting into flesh, tearing

it, and Ophion took a step back, howling in distress, one hand pressed to his chest. It hurt, burned, the injury not deep, but enough to force him to be wary. No, he wouldn't stay here, not with those sworn to Hecate. He turned, searching for any other sign of attack.

Nothing, at least for now.

He smiled, his voice calm, hands loose at his sides. No, he didn't belong here, not anymore. Not when he had a friend to protect. One who needed his assistance and he would not leave in the hands of those who would drag Petros before an unforgiving Goddess. No, his loyalty, his duty was now to those who were like him, and no other.

"Where are you going? Beast, stay with us, you do not have the right to walk away." The nearest warrior announced. "You will return with us."

He laughed, saying nothing else as he walked back toward Petros.

Someone moved, steps, heavy -- no, not cumbersome, yet he could hear them as the man rushed at him.

Ophion turned, claws extended as he lashed out at the male foolish enough to attack. Claws bit into skin, tore through muscle. A scream, pain, and terror-filled, but he continued, the second blow exposed ribs, the warrior stumbling back as he stared at Ophion.

"No, you're cursed."

If he had any other words, Ophion stole them from him with a swipe he tore out the man's throat.

They had no power over him. Not here. Not outside of their precious salt circles. No more than he could cross the ring and claim the females for himself. But there would be others, females, males, those he would gather unto himself and claim with a bite, or claw until his new family grew in numbers until not even the combined warriors of Greece would be able to stand before them.

"Not all will survive the curse, Ophion. More will die. Nor will any woman be able to breed true if they are marked by Hecate's fury." The youngest priestess called out.

"My son will never be alone again."

Ophiongrowled, turning in search of the voice. One he knew all too well. His father.

"You fool, he's dangerous. The curse is contagious. He might infect you." The second priestess warned. "You won't gain sons from him, or daughters. The curse prevents such life from taking hold, his seed is useless to you."

His father turned on the priestess and stalked toward her. "You think the continuation of my line is all I care about? Foolish female. I will protect my son, my line, my blood, no matter the cost. I will not allow you to take what is mine, destroy my family all for the sake of a too proud goddess who thinks herself more important than the gods and other males she should serve. Hecate is a fool and will pay for her pride."

Ophion grinned. "Come, father. You will be at my side."

Daichi scowled, his eyes narrowed. "I am your father, boy. Remember your place."

"I obey no one now, father. If you worked at my side, it would be best if you remember how things have now changed." He gestured at the older man. "Walk with me, or stay, I care not what you choose to do, but I will bow down to no one, not Hecate, and not you." Ophion grinned but didn't turn toward at his father, his focus once more on the man he called a friend.

On Petros.

Epilogue

"Beloved Goddess, it is done. Those sent to watch the cursed ones have returned, though not all of them survived their service to you." Two dead, both male, leaving only the two priestesses and the final guard. Alena lifted her face and looked up into the stone visage of the Goddess Hecate. She swallowed down her fears, forcing bile back down into her stomach, knowing the taste of failure. Death and the spread of the curse, this hadn't been in Hecate's plans, nor would they be able to contain the curse now it had spread beyond Athens.

"He is no longer alone. He has passed on his curse to one man, and will no doubt find others to mark. The first one will change tonight, if he hasn't already done survived the first transformation, others will wait until the next full moon." Hecate's voice warmed the chamber. "He is dangerous."

"Will we be able to protect the people of Athens should this curse grow too far, my Goddess?" Alena tried to swallow down his fear, wanting to believe in the one she would serve until her last breath. "If they spread the curse to many others, the city, and her walls, will be at risk." The punishment of one boy should not then lead to the sentence of a city, regardless of how the women were treated by their fathers, brothers, and uncles.

"I have had time to think this through. As I brought this curse into the world, then I must provide a means to defend those innocents who may be placed at risk." The Goddess paused for a moment before she continued. "You and those like you, my priestess, will alone hold the power to keep these bestial ones at bay once I have infused your blood and bodies with the skills needed. I will teach you the spells needed to confine their kind and show you how to forge a weapon which will slay them." The statue moved slightly, enough to turn Hecate so she might give her full attention to her High Priestess. "I would not leave mine own unprotected. Have faith, my servant, as long as you keep your faith you will forever be in my care."

Alena inclined her head. Faith, all she had to do was keep her faith in Hecate. "I will never turn from you." She had committed herself to the Goddess as a child, she would not -- in the face of this small challenge -- turn away from her now. "You have my devotion, my faith, and my heart. Now and always beloved Goddess."

"The listen closely, my child, and I will teach you what you need to know." The statue moved once more, stone grating, a light glowing from the carved eyes. "And there is much I need to share with you this night. You may gather the men and women who will stand against the darkness I have been foolish enough to let loose upon the lands." The figure shimmered, the Goddess parting from the stone to stand before Alena.

Power glowed from her features, filling the air, claiming stone and human alike.

Alena flinched, warmth seeping into her skin. It grew, changing from a gentle heat to a low fire and still, it continued. "My Goddess!"

"Forgive me, daughter. This must take place if you are to survive and create the children needed to fight my mistake." Hecate's voice surrounded her, keeping Alena in place. "This will... hurt, but it will be brief. Your blood is changing, adapting to the power, the gifts your daughters and their daughters will carry."

Their daughters?

Voices, familiar ones, called out in pain and fear, then calmed.

"They all must change, the men and women in this

temple, those sworn to my service, will be my weapons. My children, and the source of protection against the curse. Forgive me, child. I pray you all forgive me."

Originally from England, T.S. Weaver now lives in Minnesota with her husband and family, along with her service dog. Her work ranges from erotica and erotic romance as Terri Pray, and her non smexy work as T.S. Weaver.

When not writing she can be found with her nose stuck in a book, discussing plot lines, wrangling plot bunnies and jotting down notes on her phone to keep the idea safe.

www.terripray.com

Cursed Blood

www.ingramcontent.com/pod-product-compliance
Lightning Source LLC
Chambersburg PA
CBHW031033190726

48286CB00003BA/1149